ONE TRUE DEED

NICKEL HILL

BOOK FOUR

IRENE BENNETT BROWN

WOLFPACK
PUBLISHING
— EST 2013 —

*In memory of my uncle Roy,
soldier and Kansas cowboy.
You still inspire me.*

ONE TRUE DEED

ONE TRUE DEED

ONE

"Jocelyn, stop staring out the kitchen window. What in heaven are you looking at—and-and you're smearing raw egg on my hair?" Nila squealed. "Where's your mind?" She raised her head from the wash pan, turning a shocked smile at Jocelyn, hair dripping.

"The egg will add shine to your hair, Nila, honey." Jocelyn gently pushed her back in place. "You're going to be a beautiful bride this afternoon." Chuckling, she poured dippers of water through Nila's golden hair in a final rinse and gave her a towel. Hands on her hips, Jocelyn leaned to get a better look out the window. In the dim light of early morning, a stout stranger, a large lump in a small buggy, had halted partway up their lane, sitting with reins in his lap, staring.

"Blessed odd, should that man out there"—she pointed—"to be here for your and John's afternoon wedding, Nila. Has to be something else, but I can't imagine what." She grasped her chin and watched, feeling concern and suspicion for no sureable reason.

"Well, would you look at that? Pete comes out of the barn, aiming to talk to the stranger, looks like, and the man turns his team and buggy around. Takes off like his tailbone got scorched."

"Hmm." Nila blotted her hair with the towel, a smile playing on her face. "Maybe he was on his way somewhere and came up our lane to see as much as he could, the wedding goings on in the yard? The bower covered with leaves and flowers, rows of benches and borrowed chairs my dear 'chosen brother,' Rom, is placing?" She gave Jocelyn's shoulder a pat. "That is something, cousin, you don't see often between a house and a barnyard." She laughed. "Surrounded by cattle and horses, pigs rooting in their pen. Roosters crowing time to rise." Nila kneeled to hug Andy as the boy stumbled sleepily into the kitchen.

Joy ribboned through Jocelyn that her son, Andy, not quite six years old, would be with her and his father, Pete, for years yet. *Thank heaven.* On the other hand, Nila Malone, and the young boy, Romney Treyhern, the two youngsters that she and Pete had taken in to raise, had grown up too fast. Now in 1907, Nila was getting married, and Rom on his own working on the 101 Ranch in Oklahoma. But thank goodness, Rom was home for the wedding.

She kissed the top of Andy's head, pointed him to the table and turned back to Nila. "By the way, I've been wanting to ask something. Tell me why your two friends, when they were finishing work on your beautiful wedding dress, cut a frazzle of their hair and sewed it up in the hem? Hair in a hem. Why'd they do that? They were laughing and preening, so excited about it that I never heard why?" She placed a plate of pancakes and eggs in front of Andy, who was coming awake in his chair and picking up his fork.

"Sewing a lock of your hair into the hem of a bride's dress is a charm that guarantees you'll marry, too, within the year. My dear friend and bridesmaid, Elise Botts, would do anything to make a husband happen. As would her cousin, Maggie."

"Sweet Hannah, I never heard that one, but you'd never heard of egg in your hair, either." She quirked a grin, hands in the air. "Time's a wasting and lots still to do before folks come and you tie the knot with your handsome John Riordan." She shook her head. "I still worry about the two of you hurrying off after the ceremony, to Skiddy for the night, then clear to Europe for your honeymoon, but I know travel like that is something you've always wanted." She picked up the wash pan and headed for the door to empty it on her flowers outside.

~

*N*ila was lucky to meet and fall in love with a young man as fine as John Riordan, Jocelyn was thinking later while hurrying through the last details for today's celebration that'd follow a short but meaningful ceremony of love and promises. Putting a last swirl of icing on the wedding cake, she smiled to herself, remembering how the young couple met in a Topeka bookshop. Which wouldn't have happened at all if she and Nila hadn't made a special trip to Topeka that day for new dress material, and a brief look at books.

In the bookshop, the pair, John and Nila, had already been casting close, appraising looks at one another when he pulled a large book off a shelf and the one next to it dislodged with it and crashed down onto Nila's foot. She cried out, hopping around in pain. John, red-faced and apologetic to the core, caught her arm, held it gently, and called himself a 'stupid oaf.' Nila differed, saying she should have been more alert.

John showed his true colors with no hesitation. Kind, contrite, sympathetic, he insisted on making up for hurting her by taking the two women, Nila limping slightly, to dinner. In the process, the young people got acquainted, and having many common likes, they grew more than a little interested in one another. That was the beginning. From then on, John took every opportunity possible from his job as a journalist for the *Topeka Daily Tribune* newspaper to court Nila. Sharing mutual interests and goals, they'd fallen deeply in love, which led to today.

He had little to offer, he'd told Nila when he proposed, except for a small farm in Cloud County that his grandmother had left him, and savings in the bank.

That was plenty, Jocelyn was thinking later, their guests all seated, the couple inside the flower-bedecked bower with the minister. She sat quietly engrossed, and more than satisfied, with the minister's beautiful words regarding marriage and a loving couple's everlasting union to come. His final, "I now pronounce you man and wife and invite you to your first kiss in marriage." The latter caused the crowd to chuckle. A few fellows hurrahing, loud.

A flurry of guests left their chairs to congratulate the newly wedded couple. Pete and Jocelyn went hand in hand to hug and kiss Nila, who was more like a daughter than a cousin, and shake John's hand. "You're going to have a happy life together. I just know it," Jocelyn said.

"I don't doubt that you'll be good to our Nila," Pete added, wearing a big grin and shaking John's hand a second time.

In the heat of mid-afternoon, the newly wedded couple continued to accept congratulations from guests, chatting and smiling as they moved slowly through the crowd.

Nila's mother, Flaudie, remained constantly close by them. Gloating, introducing herself and her husband, David Clark, a decent, personable traveling salesman. *Life was so strange*, Jocelyn was thinking, studying the couple. *Mr. Clark used to be Chester Treyhern but chose to remake and improve himself, changing his name at the same time. Truth to tell, he was also Rommy Treyhern's father.* Jocelyn liked Rom's father, by whatever name he wanted to use.

She moved on, stopping for a while to listen to Rom and his friends making music with guitar, fiddle, and banjo. They struggled to play ragtime, *St. Louis Rag* in particular, which was popular, but they were without a piano or organ. She suggested that they play songs they were used to, and showing relief, they gave up and began playing "Home Sweet Home," "Red River Valley," then "Git Along Little Dogies." She covered her mouth with her handkerchief to hide her smile and walked on, did her best to ignore Flaudie, fluttering among guests, taking great effort to stress that she was Nila's mother. Never mind that she'd purposely dumped Nila, a young girl, into Jocelyn's hands to care for. Around that same time, they'd also taken in

Romney Treyhern to raise, with no objection from his father. Flaudie *was* Nila's mother, but still...

Jocelyn mentally scolded herself and shook off a tinge of hurt. She took the elbow of Mrs. Goody, her neighbor, and introduced her to Flaudie. "Mable, this is Nila's mother, Mrs. Clark. Flaudie, I'd like you to meet our dear neighbor, Mabel Goody."

Mable politely took Flaudie's hand, hesitated a trifle, then complimented Nila's mother, her expression not completely honest but trying to be kind. "I see that Nila's beauty came from you, Mrs. Clark."

Flaudie beamed, her bosom rising in pride while she poured thanks on Mabel Goody, and looked around at nearby women, trusting that they'd heard the compliment. To Jocelyn's momentary embarrassment, Flaudie centered herself in the group of women and plunged into a whispered boast about her new figure. Chiefly her bosom, which received its lovely shape from repeated application of a new product, *La Dore's Bust Food*.

Chewing the inside of her cheek in helpless disgust with Flaudie, Jocelyn shut out the woman's chatter, and standing aside, quietly surveyed the more pleasing wedding scenes around her. Andy, having a wonderful time playing tag with other youngsters his age in the yard. Closer at hand, their two fairly new cowhands, Asa 'Skeeter' Young, and Webster 'Web' Beatty were joking and laughing as they prepared to make homemade ice cream with the help of Nila's young women friends who'd been in the wedding party. The fellows hammered blocks of ice inside a burlap bag to break it up while the young women placed jars of cream and bananas alongside the freezer waiting on a makeshift table of boards on sawhorses.

Jocelyn, with a wry grin, called over to them, "I don't suppose you young folks need a hand, do you?" The girls shook their heads, faces pink, eyes dancing.

"No, thank you, ma'am, we got this taken care of just fine," Web Beatty said.

Skeeter Young answered, "Ain't never made ice cream before, but I'm learnin', Mrs. Pladson, thank you."

She laughed and kept walking.

In the short time the two cowboys had been with them on the ranch, she and Pete had grown quite fond of them. The younger one, Asa or "Skeeter" tall and thin, with a shock of sandy hair and a skimpy mustache, had been raised on his grandfather's ranch. When his grandpa Asa died, the ranch went to the bank, and he was alone. Half starved, desperately looking for work as a cowhand, he'd been directed to the Pladson ranch. They more than gladly hired him.

Soon after, they'd hired Webster, or "Web" Beatty, a short, wiry cowboy with black hair and mustache, and clear gray eyes in a brown sun-weathered face. The young fellow had been on his own since he was fifteen years old. Had run away from home in Missouri; his ma's second husband wanted him gone because Web reminded him too much of Ma's first husband, his father who'd died in jail after being beaten up in a saloon brawl—the new husband responsible for that and getting released, himself, after a few days behind bars.

Right off the young men, Web and Asa became good friends and worked well together.

Everything had changed so much. Their elderly friend, Prank Morgan, a livery stableman, passed on to heaven. Rom chose to join the 101 Ranch Show. With income from her business doings in Skiddy, mule sales and all, they'd added a good many more acres of pasture, and cattle, to Nickel Hill Ranch. They had to have more help to operate the ranch properly.

Approaching her garden, eyes on activity here and there, Jocelyn saw two of her women friends traipsing a corn row to examine the scarecrow she'd fashioned. Close by, through the open door of the barn, a group of male guests were looking over the spanking new double buggy she and Pete had recently purchased. Mostly to use for trips to town or to visit neighbors, and go to Saturday night dances. They'd still be using the wagon and her dear mules, Zenith and Alice on the ranch, for a while yet. Those mules were as hearty as ever, not surprising because working mules often lived and worked thirty to forty years. Providing they'd been given good care.

She breathed deep as a breeze rippled through tawny hayfields, lifting the summery smell of hay. She stopped suddenly, her glance catching *the same man in the buggy as earlier in the morning* coming up the lane. He drew his horse to a halt. Was he back to watch the celebration, to take part, someone they'd missed when sending invitations? Was she foolish to have this sudden cold feeling, to feel instinctively that he was an outsized bundle of trouble?

Pete headed in the direction of the stranger waiting in the buggy and Jocelyn moved to join him, only to be grabbed and pulled aside by Flaudie, who eyed Jocelyn from the waist up with a wrinkled brow. "Wait, don't leave, Jocelyn. You have to hear this." She eyed Jocelyn sympathetically, still gripping Jocelyn's arm as she continued to pontificate, "La Dore's Bust Food is *world famous.*" She turned and shook her head at a woman's question, snapping, "No, it ain't 'dangerous quackery.' You can order it from Sears. A two-ounce jar is only forty cents. There's nothing to match this bust food for its 'purity, perfume, elegance and effect.' Before using this bust cream, I was—well—scrawny, flat and flabby. Now I'm rounded, as you can see, nicely plump, my neck and arms smooth and—"

"Let go of me, Flaudie." Jocelyn shook her arm free. Skirt in hand, she hurried across the yard to the lane and Pete's side, worry like a dust devil growing in her mind.

Two

As Jocelyn grew close, the portly stranger stood up in the buggy, watching Pete's approach expectantly. Their visitor was well dressed, though in dusty and outdated clothes—a blue frock coat, silver gray vest and trousers. A weathered, flat crowned brown hat. His chubby cheeks formed a friendly smile when Pete asked, "Is there something I can do for you? I'm Pete Pladson, this is my wife, Jocelyn, Mrs. Pladson."

The man looked a trifle nervous behind his beaming smile. He held his hand out to Pete, then to Jocelyn. "Name's Lafayette." He looked around. "Nice place you folks have here."

"Did you come for the wedding, Mr. Lafayette?" Jocelyn asked. "Sorry if we missed inviting you, if so. Are you a friend of John Riordan, the groom? Or an acquaintance of some of our neighbors? The cowhands who work for us?" Should it be Prank Morgan he was here to see, the old Civil War veteran who'd operated the livery stable she'd owned and later came to live with them, she'd have to give this man sad news. The dear soul had died in his sleep the past winter.

"No ma'am, I'm here to see you folks is all." He stroked his mustache, his eyes on the crowd in the yard, plates of food in one hand and drinks in the other, the delicious aromas of roast beef and ham competing with the sunny sweet smells of Nickel Hill's grain fields.

Rom, a fully grown, broad-shouldered young man since he'd come to live with them, had joined Pete and Jocelyn, listening to the conversation. "I bet this fella would like banana ice cream and a big piece of the wedding cake, chocolate with vanilla icing. Ma is a great cook." When the stranger didn't answer, Rom pointedly asked, "Exactly what are you here for then, Mister?"

Their visitor's chin jutted, accompanied by a growl of displeasure and eyes hardening against Rom for breaking into the conversation.

"You're welcome to come for a plate and something to drink, if you want." It was difficult to relax and smile at this strange fellow, but Jocelyn managed.

He patted his oversized belly and looked longingly at the crowd feasting at the tables, as if he'd give his soul to partake of the free food. "That ain't what I came for," he finally answered, crossing his arms over his chest, a gleam in his eye as though covering a secret. "I don't want to interrupt your party over there." His meaty hand waved that way. "I come this morning, thinking to talk to you early and get it over with. Saw what was happening, thought the fuss and folderol would be over by now." He chewed his mustache, looked away from them and back defiantly.

"If not, what then?" Jocelyn, about to lose patience, encouraged clearly.

"What I come for was to have a talk about this ranch with your husband, ma'am." His gaze bore into her. "An important but unfortunate trouble you ain't going to take to. Now I'm here, I see it's best that what I got to say is left for another time." His glance measured the size of the crowd in their yard.

"Wait a minute. What in blazes are you talking about, *unfortunate trouble?* What are we not going to like?" A puzzled frown creased Pete's brow as his arm slipped around Jocelyn's waist. "Anything important you want to say about Nickel Hill, our ranch, let's have it." He waited, a bewildered, half-angry expression forming.

Lafayette, whoever he was, looked scared and belligerent at the same time. "No-sir, it can wait." He lifted his hat in a salute, clapped it back on—sending dust in the air, and took up the reins. "I'll come back in a day or two, an' we'll chew the fat when half the county ain't here." Turning his rig, shaking the reins hard, he chortled to his horse, "Get on there!" He slapped the horse into a run, clearly anxious to be away from Pete's and Jocelyn's plain-to-the-eye feelings of displeasure and distrust, Rom's snort of amusement.

The trio stood silent, watching the man roll away in a dust cloud.

"You ask me," Rom spoke up, pushing his hat further back on his head. "That man is a damned odd duck with a runaway brain."

"Rom!" Jocelyn scolded his cursing with a frown. *But who is this stranger who suddenly appears out of nowhere and gives me the shivers? About our ranch?*

Rom's young face filled with an affectionate grin at her. "Have you forgot, Ma, I've been out in the world? Rodeoing around the country with the 101 Real West Ranch Show? Believe me, I've seen his kind. He's after something and it ain't good."

"Thinking that way myself." Pete nodded. "A blowhard. That's gotta be watched."

Jocelyn, considering, took a deep breath in agreement. The man was plumb peculiar. Swept with feelings of dread at his reference to their ranch, she hooked her arm through Pete's on the walk back to the wedding party, her body as close to his side as she could get.

Later, as dark descended, only a scattered few wedding guests remained in the yard, visiting. Mrs. Goody and other women friends teamed to clean up the party leavings while Jocelyn was upstairs in the house helping Nila out of her wedding dress and into travel clothes. To Skiddy tonight, on to New York on the train, and then to Europe by steamship. "I'm going to miss you terribly--going so far, dear girl, don't you know?" Jocelyn's fingers worked at the tiny buttons down the high neck of Nila's pale pink voile wedding dress. *A lovely bride she was, the corset-like waistline showed her small waist, frills on the bodice emphasized up there.* Jocelyn smiled to herself, *no 'bust cream' needed here.* The 'Gigot' sleeves, wide and puffy, narrowed tightly to the forearm and Jocelyn tugged carefully to free Nila's arms, slipping the bridal gown to the floor in a pile of frill. Jocelyn brushed her hair back from her face. "Couldn't be happier for you, though, and you'll be back in a month, right?"

Nila, in chemise and drawers, gathered the gown

and petticoat up in her arms, not answering right away. "It could be six months to a year, Jocelyn."

Jocelyn froze, astounded. "Whyever that long, a six month honeymoon? A year?"

Nila caught Jocelyn's hand with a look of regret. "I haven't had a chance to tell you that our plans were changed at the last minute. But nothing bad. It'll be alright." She lifted a traveling suit laid out on the bed and began to dress.

"What, then?"

Nila sighed. "When John's boss at the newspaper found out that we're going to Europe, he requested John investigate situations going on over there to send back to the paper. Like covering the Young Turks Rebellion. In Turkey, of course. Other possible stories such as the London Summer Olympics that'll take place next April through October in London. John's salary would continue, working for the *Topeka Daily Tribune* during our time over there. And it'll add important credits to his work."

"I've heard a bit about the Olympic Games in London, but what, in the name of heaven, is the 'Young Turk Rebellion'? Sounds dangerous to me."

Nila, placing toiletries into a satchel, explained, her expression serious and guarded. "The rebellion is a political move, Jocelyn. A revolt or mutiny from folks against taxation and conscription, and corrupt administrators. An intent to force reforms in government. Raising arms against other parties if necessary. In this case, the younger generation against the old guard."

"A honeymoon in the middle of danger, so to speak." Her heart thudded. "I don't like the sound of it, not a little bit, Nila. Can't you say no? Talk John out of that part of your trip? I realize you've always wanted to visit other countries, Africa even, send stories that you found interesting back to America, yourself. A rebellion, though?"

"We'll be fine, we will, Jocelyn. I'll write to you as often as I can. You and Pete can look for John's name in the papers, read his stories while we're over there."

Jocelyn mumbled to herself, "Like I didn't have enough to worry about after the conversation with the nitwit today."

Nila laughed, showing relief at the change in subject. "What nitwit?"

"The stranger who showed up but never left his buggy. Telling me and Pete that he had 'unfortunate news' for us that has to do with our ranch, Nickel Hill, but he didn't want to spoil our day and he'd wait and discuss it with us another time. I think Rom was right when he said he was 'an odd duck with a runaway brain.'" She hesitated, thoughtful. "It could be that, that he's—disturbed, not of right mind. It's possible that he'll forget the matter altogether or realize that he's mistaken, that we're *not* the people or place he was looking for—I hope we've seen the last of him."

"I hope so, too, then. Now, I'd better hurry. John's waiting for me."

Jocelyn reached to hug her. "A honeymoon in Europe will be wonderful, but the rest sounds terribly unsafe to me." She stepped back. "But who am I to advise an educated, experienced, young journalist—and you, his beautiful, intelligent bride."

Nila tightened her hug. "I love you, Jocelyn. For all you've done for me, I always will." She gathered up her suitcase, satchel, and hat box, watched Jocelyn pick up the rest, and hurried for the stairs.

❧

R om had decided to spend the night and head back to Oklahoma and the 101 Ranch the next morning. Immediately after breakfast, he headed for the barn and corrals to prepare his horse and the spare mount he'd take with him. Watching from time to time from the kitchen window, half-heartedly wishing Rom was *staying here to home*, Jocelyn gathered wedding party leftovers, several ham and roast beef sandwiches, a chunk of chocolate cake carefully wrapped. She put them, with dried fruit and biscuits added, in a dish towel tied up like a sack, for him to take with him.

Outdoors later, Jocelyn, Pete, and Andy stood by watching while Rom made last preparations to go. His bedroll and canvas bag holding his clothes and personal things on the extra horse, his canteen of water, and the dishtowel containing food from his saddle. Finished, he hugged Jocelyn. "Thanks for everything, Ma. You made a right fine wedding celebration for Nila and John and I know they appreciated it. A grand time, it was, for everybody. I'm glad I came." He shook Pete's hand, then grabbed him in a quick shoulder hug. "I should stay and help you with work here at home but I really need to get back to Oklahoma if I'm going to stay on with 101."

"Don't worry about it." Pete clapped Rom on the back. "We have these two new cowhands, Skeeter and Web. Skeeter is young, just nineteen but was practically born on a horse and working with cattle, and Web is a rugged and hard-riding young gent who broke horses for a living up to now. And we always have good neighbors to help if needed."

"We're happy enough that you were able to be here for Nila's wedding," Jocelyn added quickly.

Rom's relieved grin wiped away the guilt on his face. He dug in his pocket and squatted in front of Andy to give him a shining black arrowhead. "It's yours, little brother, for luck. Don't go losing it, I brought it all the way from Oklahoma for you." He stretched a long leg out and reached again in his pocket bringing out a second arrowhead. "See, I have one, too, for luck."

Andy took his and grinned. "Thank you." He threw an arm around Rom's neck. Rom stood, ruffled Andy's hair, and headed for his horse. Andy took several slow, thoughtful steps, following. He turned. "I want to go with Rom. I can ride his extra horse. I can get some blankets and my clothes." He begged in excitement. "You gave him lots of grub. Can I go, too, please Ma? Can I, Pa?"

"Not this time, son," Pete answered.

Jocelyn made her voice light, happy. "When the 101 Real West Ranch Show comes to Kansas next time, we'll all go to see Rom and watch him ride in the rodeo, won't we?" She looked at Pete.

"Sure enough, we might even get to Oklahoma and watch him perform down there. Come on, son, stand back out of Rom's way."

Sniffling and frowning in disappointment, Andy came to stand between Pete and Jocelyn. He looked up at them. "Don't forget that you promised we'd go see him. That's what brothers are for, to see one another do stuff not everybody can do. Clap and make them feel good."

"Guaranteed, Andy, we'll go see your brother." Pete gave the boy's small shoulder a squeeze. "Now we need to finish chores."

Halfway to the barn, the trio stopped and watched Rom turn his horse south onto the main road. Missing him, already.

In the next hour, Pete saddled up and rode out to help his riders checking on cattle.

Jocelyn and Andy planted what would be a late, second crop of potatoes. Moving down the row, she dug holes in the soft dirt with her hoe, he followed, dropping a chunk or two of potato with 'eyes' in each hole. They retraced, Jocelyn hoeing dirt over them, Andy tamping the dirt down with his foot.

~

I n no time, it seemed to Jocelyn, a mountain of work was on them. Pete, their ranch hands, and a neighbor or two, were tied, dawn to dark, to the work of calving—weaning and branding. Jocelyn cooked huge noontime meals and with Andy's help, cleaned up after, along with her regular daily chores. She hardly had time to think about Nila and John and when she did, it came with worry. How were they? Was their steamship battling huge waves as they crossed the Atlantic? Were the newlyweds seasick and not able to eat?

A letter from Nila came at last. Radiating with joy, Jocelyn held the letter high as she hurried toward the house. She'd take Pete and Andy aside after dinner and read the letter to them. It wouldn't take long, and then Pete could catch up with the other workers.

She sat on the porch step and feeling breathless, read the letter.

Dear folks,

We arrived in Liverpool, Britain, yesterday. John and I are here in our hotel room to rest, but we'll be out to explore soon. A bit about our trip across the Atlantic. We were fortunate to travel on the enormous and beautiful British steamship Lusitania which was making its return trip to the United Kingdom. Can you imagine, it has six decks?

Oh, yes, the Lusitania is a fast steamship, its turbine engines allowed speed at 29 miles an hour! We chose second-class passage and were most comfortable. First-class deck furnishings are said to be sumptuous, second-class plainer and simpler, but to us everything was grand. I was envious, though, that the reading and writing room was for first-class passengers only. No matter, John and I enjoyed sitting outside on the deck viewing the scenery, and taking walks on the promenade deck, stopping now and then to visit with other passengers. That is, we did when the liner wasn't pitching forward making huge waves. We've experienced only a touch of seasickness.

The luncheon menu is far too tempting. 'Lamb pot pie or roast beef or roast chicken.' If the diner prefers cold food, there is 'London pressed beef, galantine of turkey with aspic jelly, endive, and tomatoes.' Desserts can be fancy pastry, jam pudding, or a compote of prunes and rice.

*Thinking of you all with much love. I'll write
again as soon as I can. John and I will take a few
days for our honeymoon sightseeing, then he must
get down to business—with my help. Ha.*

Sincerely,
Nila and John Riordan

Jocelyn smiled, wiped her eyes, and with the letter
clasped to her chest, hurried inside to fix dinner.

Weeks passed and the stranger, Lafayette, whatever
he'd been up to, hadn't returned. Jocelyn was relieved,
heart and soul. One evening after supper, she
mentioned the matter to Pete. "I hope this Lafayette
person will never be back, whatever 'seriousness' might
be on his mind against Nickel Hill and us."

"Time to forget it," Pete said. "Probably didn't
amount to anything, anyway."

The weather at home on the ranch became hotter
with deep summer, and Andy had chosen to shed his
shoes until fall and go barefoot. Playing around the barn
one day, he stepped on an old rusty, hand-wrought,
square nail, painfully injuring his foot. He hadn't told
Jocelyn about it at first, and an infection set in until
walking on the foot had become impossible. Jocelyn
wrung her hands while warming milk to make a bread
and milk poultice for his foot. "Son, you need to tell me
about something like this as soon as it happens. You let
it go and it will get infected, like it has now." She'd
heard too many stories about such an infection turning
to gangrene and costing a leg, but she couldn't share
that.

He wiped at tears on his dusty face. "I washed it at

the pump by the barn 'til it was clean an' it felt better. I didn't know no infection would happen." He scowled. "Make it all swelled up and sore as h—"

She held up a hand. "Right there, stop Andy. I don't care how many swear words you hear from menfolk around here, you're not to repeat them. Now then, let me soak some bread in warm milk and make a poultice to wrap onto your foot. That will draw the pus out and make your foot better. We'll do it again, often as we have to, until your poor foot heals." She hummed a little tune about 'wiping her worries away' while wrapping his foot. It didn't help much.

A short time later, there was the sound of an arriving horse outside. She looked out the window. Her heart began to hammer. *He was back, this person, wanting to make trouble, Lafayette.* Pete, who'd been working at the barn, had seen him, too, and was heading in the direction of the man waiting in his buggy. She turned to her son, helped him to the sofa in the front room. "I want you to rest, off your foot, Andy." She handed him the book he'd been reading, Rudyard Kipling's Just So Stories. "Read this for a while, or one of your other books. A nap would be good, too. I'm going outside to talk with Daddy for a while." She hurried, her heart thumping with dread.

THREE

The visitor frowned in Jocelyn's direction and shook his head as she hurried to Pete's side. Lafayette growled at Pete, "I want to talk to you alone, Mr. Pladson. If you don't mind, ma'am"—he flipped his hand—"you can go on back to the house an' your work. No need to worry your head about this." He licked his lips nervously. "It's a man's matter about this property, the ranch."

The more he tried to be rid of her, the more Jocelyn determined not to move an iota.

Pete spoke quietly, a glitter of anger in his eyes. He was blunt. "The hell you say, Mr. Lafayette. She stays. We wouldn't have Nickel Hill Ranch in the first place, if not for Jocelyn here, my wife."

She smiled thanks at Pete and waited, hands clasped in front of her to keep them still.

He needn't've put it that way, but it was fact. Whit Hanley, her boss at one time, and his mother, too, were good friends of hers. Whit was killed by an outlaw, leaving Nickel Hill Ranch to his mother, Francina

Gorham. Francina had left the ranch to her and Pete, in her will. That was final and sure.

"What I got to tell you all, then—" He cleared his throat. "Is that this ranch is not yours. Not legally."

"That can't be," Jocelyn and Pete said in unison. They frowned at one another, puzzled.

"It is. Hate to have to tell ya." His tone and expression gave lie, with a touch of nervousness to his words. "My full name is Lafayette Hanley. Or you can call me Lafe Hanley. I am a younger half-brother to a man I believe you maybe knew at one time, Whit Hanley? My pa was Whitman Hanley senior, me born to his second wife."

Jocelyn, fists clenched, was too stunned to speak. "I knew Whit Hanley, Junior," she was finally able to say, "A good man, my boss at one time on a mule drive. I was with him when he died, shot and killed by an outlaw." She experienced a deep sadness, remembering.

"I heard about that," Lafayette, or 'Lafe' quickly agreed. "My pa, the senior Hanley, originally bought this place here, from Matilda Scott, a widow. Her husband, Emmett, had died a'ready. When my half-brother, Whit Hanley, Jr., died in that gunfight, I guess was when his pa—my pa changed his will, leaving this ranch to me. Not to the wife he divorced, Whit Jr.'s Ma, who, from what I've learned, just handed it over to you like it had belonged to her." He added quickly, "Uh, Pa —never willed it to his second wife, neither, that'd be my ma." He sat up straighter, looking half scared, yet a smile forming on his chubby cheeks, his mustache rising. "This place"—he waved an arm with an expression full of anxious greed—"is my rightful property." He swallowed. "Every bit of it."

"The hell it is!" Pete exploded, glaring at him. He laughed. "Are you joking, Mister, or what?"

Lafayette, his eyes darting with fear at Pete, leaned away on the buggy seat and grunted, "I know how you probably feel, but that ain't my problem. You folks'll have to find another location to settle." He swallowed. "That's all. You gotta leave. This ranch is mine."

Jocelyn looked him in the eye. "You're dead wrong, Mr. Lafayette, whoever you may be. This property became Francina Hanley Gorham's when Whit, her son, was killed, and according to papers he left for her. As a young man, he'd led a shaky life with an outlaw gang, and he wanted this ranch to go to his mother if anything happened to him. That is that. Your word is in direct conflict with our legal papers. *Legally willed title to Nickel Hill Ranch*," Jocelyn emphasized. "Wait right here, don't you move this buggy one inch. I can show you the deed."

Instead of handing it to him to read when she returned, Jocelyn held the document up a moment or two for him to see, and then she read aloud:

> *"This Indenture, executed as a Deed, Made the 15th day of October AD, 1901 between Francina Hanley Gorham of Topeka, Kansas, party of the first part, and Jocelyn Pladson and Pete Pladson of Skiddy, Kansas, parties of the second part, WITNESSETH, That the said party of the first part for and in consideration of the sum of One Dollar to her hand, paid by the parties of the second part, the receipt whereof is hereby acknowledged to grant that tract of land lying in the county*

of Morris, and state of Kansas and described as
follows, to wit—"

"I know what you got here, two thousand acres. I can see it for my own eyes," Lafayette barked. "And I don't need to hear no more gibberish."

"I want to finish." Jocelyn moistened her lips. "With the end at least." She raised her voice several notches to perfectly clear,

> *"The above granted lands and premises, in the quiet and peaceful possession of the said parties of the second part, their heirs and assigns, against all persons lawfully claiming, or to claim, the whole or any part thereof, the said party of the first part will warrant and defend.*
> *IN TESTIMONY THEREOF, The said party of the first part has hereunto set her hand and seal the day and year first above written. FRANCINA HANLEY GORHAM.*
> *Signed Sealed And Delivered In The Presence of THEODORE ARCHER, Notary Public."*

She smiled. "There you are, simple and perfectly legal. That settles it."

He roared, "Don't settle nothin' when it's willed to me, too. Give the damn thing here. I'll rip—" He grabbed at the deed.

Jocelyn yanked it back, losing a corner of the document to his beefy fist.

In a flash Pete had Lafayette's shirt front gripped in his fist. Lafayette's face swelled and turned red, he began to cough, trying to breathe. Pete let him go.

"We're having a discussion here, and you treat my wife like the good woman she is or else." He waited, hands on his hips. "Are you finished here, or not?"

Breathing hard, Lafayette straightened his collar and shook his head. "My pa, Whitman Hanley the first," he blustered, "died of a heart attack several years ago. I got a letter about that, with a newspaper clipping of the obituary. But I learned only recently that his properties were meant for his descendants." He licked his lips. "Which is me, the only one left. I been travelin' a lot the last few years. To Missouri and back, Wyoming, Texas. Working every job from barkeep to sheep herder, to baker and more." His expression soured then quickly brightened. "I was tickled pink—uh sorry to hear he'd died, though—that he named me in line to have this property. It ain't my fault, folks"—he pulled a handkerchief from a vest pocket and mopped his sweating face—"but you have to go."

Jocelyn felt her heart had stopped. She looked at Pete in question.

"You've got proof to show us that Nickel Hill belongs to you, too, right here, now?" Pete demanded to know.

"Oh, I got it, yes. Yeah, I got proof, fer sure." He wiped his face with a grungy handkerchief. "I got papers. Didn't bring them with me this time, want to keep them safe. I just wanted you to know early, give you folks time to leave, let you down easy." He gave them a shallow grin.

"We're not leaving," Jocelyn said, despite cold fear. "Not until we've had a chance to look further into this crazy situation for ourselves."

Pete, his jaw clenched, said, "Yeah, and if we have

to, we'll get the best damn lawyer we can find. But that won't be necessary, Nickel Hill Ranch is ours. In the meantime I have work to do." He turned away.

"You'll move off here when I say"—Lafayette lifted a fist in a fury—"if I have to get the sheriff and a whole posse onto you."

"Bring 'em, we're not leaving," Pete shouted over his shoulder.

After Lafayette—it was hard to refer to him as Mr. Hanley—rolled away in a dust cloud, Jocelyn looked around, feeling hollow and worried, surveying all they'd have to leave if what this odd person said turned out to be true. *Two* deeds? How could that be? They couldn't lose Nickel Hill, after all the work they'd done. What making a life here meant to them. They couldn't. Something had to be done to fix this...soon.

~

"We still own the property in town where the livery used to be," Jocelyn told their cow, Trudy, her forehead against the critter's flank as she milked. Other than the rhythmic spang of milk into the bucket and her cow's occasional rustling move and stomp of a hoof, early morning inside the barn was a quiet, peaceful place where she could think. "Trouble is, I still need the town property for mule sales and rental pasturage."

Sweet Hannah, am I sharing my troubles with my Trudy cow? Ah, well... "There would only be room for a small house if we built one there and I wouldn't like living in town a quarter as much as I do here at the ranch." Trudy rumbled in her throat and waggled her short horns. "See, you do agree. Nickel Hill will always be home to Pete, Andy, and me. And you, Trudy, old as you're getting to be. Then, too, it'll always be a place where Nila and Rom will feel most comfortable when they come to visit. Home."

She stood, finally, hefting the bucket of foaming milk and scooting the milking stool aside with her foot. "I know what I have to do, talk to Francina's attorney, that's what. Find out if there's anything suspicious in any of her legal papers, before us. If he still has them." Her worry lifted a little as she released Trudy from the stanchion and sent her out of the barn into the back pasture.

"I know you're tired, Pete," she told him that evening as she cleared away supper dishes. "But we need to talk about this Lafayette 'Hanley' situation."

"We do. I heard you spilling your troubles to your milk cow today, of all the damn things." He grinned, shook his head and nodded toward the porch. "Let's go out and sit where it's cooler."

They dropped into twin rockers and looked at one another. Jocelyn took the lead. "Do you think by some mistake two deeds to Nickel Hill actually exist? One from Whit's father's will *and* a second from his mother, Francina's? Our deed?"

He leaned his head back in his rocker and tiredly mopped a hand down his face. "Hell, hon, I hardly know what to think. First off, I wouldn't trust this fella who says he is a Hanley to pet my dog if I had one. I figure that he's either lying or he's cooked up some scheme to get the place, half legal, maybe. All in all, I feel he's crooked as they come, that, or a few wires loose upstairs." He sleepily tapped his temple.

She nodded. "It seems that way to me, too. Unless there's some happenstance we've not been able to come up with." After a long silence, Pete's eyes remained closed, having fallen asleep. Jocelyn reached to touch his arm, and he jumped.

"What?"

"Sorry, sweetheart, I'll let you go to bed in a minute. We can't wait longer to talk to a lawyer, Pete, preferably Francina's attorney, Abel Paggett. We met him after Francina's funeral when he read the will, remember? He would know, surely if anyone does, whether we're in serious trouble or not." *If we've lost our home, our ranch, left with nothing*. With that thought, she felt deeply hollow.

"I can't hardly leave the ranch in the middle of haying, Jocelyn. Unless I—"

"You don't have to leave, Pete. I'll go to Topeka and look Mr. Paggett up as soon as Andy's foot's better, so I can take him with me."

"Did you try calling Paggett on the new telephone, talk this over? I thought you were going to a few days ago?"

Her mouth dried, and she nodded. "I tried calling but the number we have is from almost two years ago. The people I talked to at that number had no idea who he was, even. I thought that if I went to Topeka, I might locate people we met at the funeral, the minister, or the funeral director who'd know where I could find him, if he's settled in a different town. If none of that works"— she scratched the side of her nose—"I'll take our trouble to the young attorney, Grant Sanborn, who represented Herman Taggert at his trial over the troubles his mother gave us, cattle rustling and trying to burn us out. I really liked Sanborn, didn't you?" She sat forward, stilling her rocker, not waiting for an answer. "Or Judge Rawlins, at Council Grove. One way or the other, I intend to solve this, and with honesty winning, it will end in our favor. Be over with." She sat back, rocking, nodding with confidence that she was on the right path.

Pete stood up a few minutes later, stretched, and came to kiss her forehead. "If anyone can straighten this out, you and our Andy can. But that's for another day. C'mon, let's go to bed."

She laughed softly. "I'm glad you feel it's alright that I go. I'm giving Andy's foot another few days, and then we're catching the train in Skiddy and heading to Topeka."

As she knew he would be, Andy was thrilled with the three-hour train ride, his face glued to the train window. Especially when they came through a small town new to him, his attention was captured by people coming and going on sidewalks and into the stores. In one town, he spotted a colorful circus in a large field with a busy Ferris Wheel, merry-go-round and performing elephants. He turned, looking over his shoulder until the circus disappeared from sight and then sat back with a sigh of pleasure.

On arrival, she took his hand, and they caught the streetcar to the funeral home that had provided Francina's funeral service and burial. His excitement fell away when they entered the cool and solemn quiet of the funeral parlor and he looked around, his face glum.

"Wait here, son." She pointed to a chair outside the office marked Funeral Director. "I won't be long."

"I don't like it here, Momma," he whispered like a young ghost as he sat down.

Jocelyn hesitated, thinking it over. "Alright, Andy, come in with me."

He stood up slowly. "Are there dead people in there?" He lowered his head, his eyes suspiciously on the door.

"No, son, this is just an office. We'll find out what we need to know, and that will be all." She pressed a finger to her lips. "But Momma will do the talking."

After a long discussion about Francina's funeral and a-sundry other things, like the June flood with rowboats the main transportation around Topeka. The heat of summer and early fall that followed, and—for Andy's sake, discussion of the wonderful yellow brick road being built to Dorothy's House in Liberal, Kansas. Jocelyn spoke up, "We have the book, THE WONDERFUL WORLD OF OZ, written, I believe, in 1900 by Frank Baum. We'd love to go to Liberal and see the yellow brick road, wouldn't we, Andy?"

"I think so. Yeah, I would." He nodded. "If the Scarecrow and Tin Man are there—and yeah, Dorothy," he added out of the corner of his mouth. His eyes widened. "And the Wicked Witch ain't."

"Isn't, son," Jocelyn corrected. *How on earth did they get sidetracked?*

"Ah yes, Frank Baum, I met him when we both were traveling salesmen before he wrote *The Wonderful World of Oz* and I became a funeral director. We became friends. He's a very interesting fellow. Before he wrote that magnificent book, he raised prize-winning chickens, published a trade journal, was an actor and playwright. He moved his family to Aberdeen, South Dakota Territory and opened a novelty goods store he called Baum's Bazaar. When that failed due to a serious drought, he became owner of the local newspaper. Many editorials he penned championed women's rights. His mother-in-law, Matilda Gage, you know, was a leader in the women's rights movement."

"I didn't know that. Good for him. And his mother-in-law. I've been engaged in the women's rights movement myself, at times."

Andy wasn't as interested in the funeral director's conversation as Jocelyn was and he began to squirm. Jocelyn opened her mouth, hoping to return to her subject, Attorney Abel Paggett, when the gentleman in charge continued, "When Baum began writing children's books, many of his main characters were tenacious, self-reliant girls."

"Really? That is truly wonderful. Girls are so often overlooked in many ways." Andy was yanking on Jocelyn's hand, wanting to leave, but all this information was interesting to her.

The funeral director finally noticed Andy's squirming. "Turned out that Frank Baum's first bestseller, published in 1899, was also a children's book, *Father Goose, His Book*. You might want to read that, too, young man." He looked at Jocelyn. "Sorry we got off track there for a few minutes. I wish I had information about Francina Gorham's attorney, Abel Paggett, but I don't. Other than a rumor that he's left Topeka and took his practice elsewhere. He could've left the state, but it's also possible he's still in Kansas. Wichita, or

Manhattan, maybe. I just don't know. Tell you what, I'll give you the name and address of the minister who conducted the service. It's possible that he might have information that'll help you, Mrs. Pladson."

"Thank you, sir, I'd appreciate it."

After a long, perspiring walk up one street and then another, Jocelyn, Andy in hand, located the minister in his parsonage next to the church. Seated in his sparsely furnished parlor, having offered something to drink, water or iced tea, he kindly gave Jocelyn his full attention. In between sips of tea, Jocelyn related her and Pete's mixed-up deed troubles. "It's very important that I find Attorney Pagett to help clear the matter once and for all." *And their worries turned to naught.*

With his hands clasped in front of him, the minister rocked back and forth on his heels, his eyes squinting in thought. "Unfortunately, I'm not able to tell you where Attorney Paggett is." He gave her a studious look, nodded, and then smiled. "It's possible that our organist, who played the organ for Mrs. Gorham's funeral, might have some idea of Attorney Paggett's whereabouts. Excuse me, please." He turned to his desk, pulled open a drawer for a pen, small bottle of ink, and paper. "This is the organ lady's address." He finished writing and gave Jocelyn the slip of paper. "I pray that this will complete your search."

She took a deep breath. "Thank you so much, Reverend. I hope so, too." *Desperately hope so.*

FOUR

Andy loved being outside again and was in awe of all the activity and sights of the city. Jocelyn, doing her best to shake off disappointment as they walked along, hummed the song, "All Things Bright and Beautiful," the happy song Francina had personally requested be played and sang at her funeral. After walking five blocks to the organ lady's house, Andy's foot was beginning to bother him a bit. And the organ lady, who liked to talk about a bit of everything, even playing Francina's song for them, couldn't provide an iota of help in finding Paggett, either.

They stood outside the organist's house, Jocelyn's shoulders slumped and trying to think what to do next while Andy stood on one foot, lifting the injured one off the brick walk. *We've spent too long here in the city and no luck at all! And Andy's sore foot bothering him more by the minute.* She pressed her lips tight, then said, "Tell you what, son, we're taking the streetcar back to the train station and we'll find a place to eat nearby.

Then we'll wait for the train. We're going home. I'm so sorry about your foot, Andy. We should've stayed home on the ranch."

"It's alright, Momma, it don't hurt that bad. But my foot wants to go home, too."

"Good enough." She kissed the top of his head. She'd be more than happy to leave the train at Skiddy, pick up their team and buggy at the livery, and head to the ranch.

~

Jocelyn reined the team and buggy to a stop before the house the same time Pete leaped from the dark of the porch to meet them. Taking her by the waist and helping her down, he said, "Sure glad to see you two home safe." He looked at her in the dim light, his brow deeply wrinkled and his tone ragged. "That jackass was here again this afternoon." He caught Andy scrambling out of the buggy and helped him gently to the ground due to his foot and looked again at Jocelyn.

"Who was here?" Jocelyn asked, heaving a weary sigh. "Please don't tell me that it was that Lafayette person—and if so, I'd prefer you not insult our mules calling Lafayette a jack—well, you know."

"Yes, him."

"Did he bring the deed he claims to have this time?"

"He might've. I don't know if he did or not, because we didn't talk. I was out in the field cutting rye, when I looked up and saw him. Dumb fool waved for me to come from the field to him. Damned if I would, if he was too lazy to get his fat rear out of his rig. Darn fool might've been afraid of what I'd do to him if he faced me on my sod, an' he'd be right." The two horses stomped impatiently in the dust and tried to reach a grassy area. Pete took the lines and motioned with his head. "Go on in the house with Andy, sweetheart. I'll be in after I unhitch and get this team and watered an' you can tell me what you found out."

Later, as they prepared for bed, Jocelyn did her best to keep weariness and disappointment from her voice and gave Pete the details of her and Andy's day. "It was all for nothing." She smiled grimly despite wanting to do otherwise. "My hopes to find and talk to Francina's attorney." Continuing, her spirits rose a trifle. "Not for Andy, though. He loved the train ride there, then the busy city, riding the electric streetcar down the middle of the street, horse traffic on both sides. The biggest thrill for him was the horse-drawn, steam-powered noisy fire engine racing toward a fire, steam clouds billowing behind them."

"You two weren't in danger, I hope."

"We weren't. The fire was on Quincy Street, I heard, and hopefully not major. At a restaurant and bakery, while waiting for the train, we took rest at a small table and had hot chicken soup. And delicious frosted orange sponge cake for dessert. We brought a couple slices for you."

She slipped her nightgown down over her head and sat down at her dressing table, braiding her hair. "In the morning I'm going to telephone Olympia Stewart, she lived with Francina for years and they were close friends. I'd like to know her feelings about Francina's will, should she be aware of anything valuable to us about it. I'm praying that she'll be able to help." She looked over her shoulder at Pete. "I want to find out where we stand for sure with our deed, before that fool pest, Lafayette, shows up again—if he does and he probably will."

The next day, as Jocelyn went about her daily chores, feeding the chickens, milking Trudy the cow, preparing breakfast, making beds, redding the kitchen, planning dinner, heating water on the stove to wash clothes, she took an occasional time out to try and reach Olympia Stewart on the wall telephone in the living room. Each time, the party line was busy with women exchanging recipes, chatting up gossip about a neighbor, arguing over recent newspaper stories—there was no end to it. On her final try, it occurred to her that if she did finally reach Olympia, hordes of eavesdroppers would be listening in on every word they said. News of their trouble from the odd stranger, claiming to be the true owner of their ranch, would spread like wildfire throughout the county, the state, from women's mouths in a flash of seconds.

She gave up, thinking, *I'd best write a letter. I prefer that anyway, to talking on the telephone. It's fair certain that a letter will reach Olympia in Indiana at her daughter's home, sooner than I can find the telephone party line open and available.*

～

An answer to her letter came speedily enough.

Dearest Jocelyn,

> *To answer your question, yes, I know about young Whitman's will to his mother, and her will*

*to you and Pete. Both documents were completely
proper and legal in every way. Francina never
cared for bookwork or numbers. I was her helper,
good friend, and companion in all respects. I often
served as something of a secretary, helping her pay
bills, keep track of affairs at the bank, everything
like that. I was present when her lawyer, Abel
Paggett helped her draw up the will. I recall him
saying that her son Whitman was the only owner
of the property, left to him by his father, as well as
Francina was the only one from young Whitman's
will to her. I saw both documents as I took them to
the bank to place in her safety deposit box. If there
is such a thing as another deed around for the same
property, my guess is that it's a fake, or a terrible
mistake. Yours and Pete's deed, signed and given to
you by the Notary Public, is the only one and true
deed to Nickel Hill Ranch, I'm positive.*

*P.S. One more thing, you said in your letter
that you tried to locate Abel Paggett, the attorney,
in Topeka. Sorry to tell you that he is not in Kansas
anymore. He took his practice to Colorado, but I
don't know where in Colorado. I wish you every
possible iota of good luck!"*

Yours sincerely, Olympia Stewart

Jocelyn lifted the letter to her lips, grateful
beyond measure to have this bit of proof that Nickel
Hill Ranch was theirs. Now to prove that this was
'the only true deed.' Put it away safely to start. But
where? In a safety deposit box at the bank? She
supposed so, but she hated the thought of letting the

paperwork out of her sight knowing what 'Lafayette whomever' might be up to. She couldn't do that, not just yet. In no way could they lose their ranch, not ever.

As soon as she had an opportunity, Jocelyn explained their worrisome situation to Attorney Grant Sanborn, the dark-haired, wise young man who'd so wonderfully handled the Herman Taggert trial, a major concern from her and Pete's past. She handed their Nickel Hill Ranch deed across the desk to him. Luckily, she'd thought his office was in Council Grove, it had turned out that his location was in White City, closer to home. She waited, breath caught in her throat as he studied the form, the ticking of his office clock seeming unnaturally loud.

"A deed"—his eyes lifted to her with a smile—"must meet the common law requirements to be valid and enforceable." His attention returned to the precious document in his hand. "Let me see now—yes, the grantor, Francina Hanley Gorham, had the legal ability to grant the property. That's accordingly signed here by credible witnesses. Hmm, yes, the grantor, Mrs. Gorham, gave general warranty of title against any future claims. Good that she included that. The deed was delivered to and accepted by you and your husband, the *grantees*. And—I see here, the two of you saw that the deed was properly recorded. Most important." The paper crackled as he scanned it a second time, line by line. The silence seemed to last forever to Jocelyn. "Mrs. Pladson, you have nothing to worry about. This legal document is undeniable proof that you and your husband are the true owners of the ranch. The other person claiming a right to the property is a fraud and a possible danger." He gave her the deed. "Have you talked to the law about him?"

"Yes, I have." She'd gone to Skiddy for groceries and other supplies and while there stopped to see Marshal Hillis. He'd told her that if the culprit showed up again, to let him know and he'd take care of the matter. In the meantime, keep their doors locked and keep an eye out for trouble. He'd also provided the information she needed to find Grant Sanborn's location. That being White City, she'd be home in fair time to tell Pete the news that they were indeed the only owners of Nickel Hill.

Sanborn waved away her offered payment and saw her to the door. "Today is just an introduction. If we had to go to court, that would be different." He tapped his lips with his forefinger, cupped his elbow with the other hand. "I'd sure like to look at the copy of the will the scoundrel says he has, if there is such a thing."

"I would, too. On the other hand, I hope to never see nor hear of him again."

"Can't blame you for that." He smiled.

"Thank you so much, Mr. Sanborn. I'm glad this didn't take long. My son Andy is waiting outside in our buggy, gobbling ginger cookies and looking through a book called THE RELUCTANT DRAGON. A favorite book of Pete's when he was a young boy."

He laughed. "As it should be. Give Pete and the boy my regards."

"I'll do that."

A lthough their own will was legitimate proof that they owned Nickel Hill, Jocelyn couldn't help but wonder if there was, by some mistake, a second will. It was hard to dismiss the possibility of a second wife to the elder Whitman and a half-brother to her friend and boss, the younger Whit. Grant Sanborn had said he'd like to look into that, himself. He'd check it out.

It was weeks later that a letter came from Attorney Sanborn, saying that he could find no record of Whitman Hanley Sr. marrying a second time. Although he did have a lady friend who was caring for him through an illness until he died. Nor was there any indication of a half-brother. The only information he uncovered was record of a legal will leaving the elder Hanley's holdings, the large Nickel Hill Ranch, to Whitman Hanley Junior. And Mrs. Gorham's will to them. Jocelyn was elated.

She and Pete were breathing easy, having decided that they'd seen the last of the so-called Lafayette Hanley, when his buggy came rolling up the lane again. Both went out to stop him where he was and let him know the facts. Before he had a chance to bring up his useless, irritating, time-wasting ramble again.

Jocelyn looked up at Pete, caught his arm, signaling that she'd like to be the one to tell Lafayette the facts of their deed. Seated in the buggy, he looked bored, did his best to appear he had no interest in anything they had to say.

She smiled calmly and began, looking him squarely in the eyes. "I had our deed examined by an excellent lawyer and he's assured us that the document is in every way legal and Nickel Hill most definitely belongs to us.

Pete and me, only." She hesitated, looking for his reaction. He waved her words away. She continued, speaking clearly. "Lawyer Sanborn searched very carefully but found no record of a second marriage for the elder Hanley, Whit's father. And not a whisper of information to existence of a half-brother." She waited. Pete grinned from ear to ear.

"The hell you say," Lafayette retorted, surprising them with a triumphant expression. "Here's my lawyered deed, ma'am. You take a look at it, and you'll see how wrong you folks are."

Frowning but still confident they were in the right, Jocelyn stepped forward and accepted the smudged, much-handled sheet of paper, one hand on her chin and feeling deep doubt. She looked it over carefully, concentrating on every word. For the most part, it was a properly filled out form—that he'd probably gotten from a commercial printing business that provided legal blanks, such as she'd seen in Topeka.

"This looks fine." She held the paper up. "Except for a couple of important things left out." She breathed deep, filled with satisfaction. "There are no witnesses' signatures to attest to the legality of this grant of property. No indication that this so-called deed has been recorded, either. This is just words on paper." She held the paper up to him. "Did you find a crooked lawyer to write this fake deed up for you? By some means, force him to do this if he was an honest lawyer? There's no name or address of any official on here. Did he purposely leave off that information to clear himself? And leave you the guilty one?"

"Don't matter, none of your mouthy squirrel clatter. I ain't guilty of nothing." He snatched the paper back.

"This place is my property and there ain't anything you can do to stop me from having it. You better be moving out 'cause I'm moving in."

"You sure as hell won't." Pete looked at him in disgust, barely containing his impatience. "You've given us enough trouble, now git, and don't *ever* show up here at Nickel Hill Ranch again. You hear me? *Never*."

Jocelyn warned Lafayette, "I've told Marshal Leo Hillis about you trying to steal our property and continuing to make trouble for us. He said to report you if you came again with this false nonsense. We have a telephone in the house, and I'm going to use it, right now, to report you and what you're attempting."

"Won't do you no good," he blustered, his eyes holding a shade of worry. "I been treating you nice enough, giving you a chance to face up to the fact this place is mine and you need to leave. I'll bring a shotgun next time I come and if y'all ain't out of here, I'll use it."

"We'll be here. We have had enough of you, so stop being a damn nuisance." Pete ground out, "And you'll not be the only one armed. You show up, and I'll pepper-shoot you plumb to Colorado." He motioned his head toward the road.

Lafayette's nostrils flared in anger. He spat over the side of his buggy and whipped the horse, turning the rig wide in the lane, the left front wheel wobbling slightly. "You folks don't know how bad I can make things for you with some help I got coming," he said over his shoulder. "But you'll be finding out, and you'll beg to leave."

Jocelyn looked at Pete, feeling numb, her hands jammed into fists in her apron pockets.

His harsh squint followed the departing buggy.

"That man is crazy as all get out. I ought to have hauled him out of that buggy and beat the holy hell out of him."

"Hope you don't have to. I'm reporting him. It's best we turn this over to the law."

~

Harvest time was full on them. Everyone at the ranch busy from the first shred of dawn to deep dark. On occasion, Lafayette was spotted in his buggy, halted out on the road at the far end of their lane. He was ignored by mutual decision between Jocelyn and Pete, and their help. It wasn't easy. Sometimes he sat there for an hour or more before giving up and turning back down the main road. Marshal Hillis had ordered him to stay away from Nickel Hill Ranch or be charged with illegal trespassing. Even so, he seemed determined to give them the bad eye from a distance, a warning of worse to come.

Counter to the almost constant irritation Lafayette caused, were a flurry of joy-filled letters from Nila. Most were short but included pictures of their hotels and other ancient, awe-inspiring architecture. Street scenes and dining in quaint cafes, trying dishes that they'd never, ever had growing up in Kansas. The young couple was having a wonderful adventure and Jocelyn couldn't be happier for them.

An even briefer note came from Rom but was equally welcome:

*I miss home and being with y'all there at the
ranch but I sure like it here, too, in Oklahoma and*

getting to ride in a rodeo every now and then.
Which is why I'm writing you now. There is a
chance we'll be bringing an offshoot of the big
101 Real West Show to somewhere in Kansas,
and I sure want you to come. I'll let you know
later exactly where it will be. See you all
then, Rom.

A few days later, Jocelyn took time out from work at home for a trip to Skiddy and business matters there. She drew her team and buggy to a stop in front of her large stock barn, remainder of where her livery stable also used to be, before a gang of no-goods destroyed it. Climbing from the buggy, she was surprised to see a herd of goats in a small pen. Likely left over from a stock sale that her business partner, George Jacobsen, had held and she had to miss due to other goings on at the ranch. She also rented pasture here on the property, and taking a walk, she saw several milk cows—probably owned by town folk, and in another area, three horses and a few mules.

Content with what she saw, she headed her rig toward the outskirts of town to the feedstore and the new livery to talk with George and catch up on their business doings.

"I'm sorry I've missed the last two mule sales, George, but this summer's been packed full of everything you could think of, from holding a wedding out there on the ranch and a hoodlum idiot trying to tell us we don't own the farm fair and square, that he does."

"You're not joking, are you?" George looked at her in disbelief, a crooked half-smile on his face.

She explained the situation about Lafayette while

George continually shook his head and exclaimed, "Nah—that can't be—you got to be kidding."

"It's the god-awful truth, all of it, George. It's no joke." She threw up her hands. "Now let's talk about the business, and again, I'm sorry I haven't been here to help."

He led her into his small office in the feedstore and showed her the books. "We've been doing pretty fine, as you can see. I have checks for you from the rental of your sale barn, the sales, and rent checks for the pastures." He opened a drawer and gave them to her.

"Thank you, George. I never imagined, when those outlaws wrecked my livery, I'd be doing this well as a result." She put the money in her beaded handbag and shook his hand. "Now, I need to have a talk with the marshal."

FIVE

Jocelyn spotted the town marshal on the street as she was headed toward his office. She hurried forward, telling him that Lafayette's pesky visits hadn't stopped, although he hung back from a distance on the road at the end of their drive. Ignoring him hadn't helped much, but they were glad that he was too cowardly to come face them on their home ground with his threats.

"I found where he's staying now by asking around," the marshal told her, removing his hat and waving it. "He's squatted yonder a few miles outside town, an abandoned shack in a gully of cedar trees."

"Good." She bit her lip. "You've talked to him?"

"I have, but I didn't know that he was still hanging around out your way. Glad you told me." His brow deepened in a frown. "I warned him. No telling what the fool has on his mind." He turned away, leaned from the sidewalk and spat angrily into the dusty street, slapped his leg with his hat and then put it back on. "I'll put a stop to this, once and for all. Don't you worry, Mrs. Pladson. I'll take care of this ornery scum."

It was steaming hot several days later when Marshal Hillis came out to the ranch to report to Jocelyn and Pete, the three of them seated on the porch in the shade. "When I told him I'd heard from you, Jocelyn, that he was still coming back here, he said you were lying." He pulled a handkerchief from his pocket and mopped his face. "Said that it was none of my business if he did, that I didn't own the main road, if he wanted to stop somewhere on it. The blamed scoundrel continued to argue with me, called me names, tried booting me in the face from up there in his buggy."

"Goodness, no." Jocelyn stiffened in protest.

"That did it. I yanked him off that buggy seat—took both hands and a lot of pull—he's so heavy. He kicked and punched me before I could get my breath. I finally got the fat ox down, handcuffed him, and told him that I was charging him with assaulting an officer of the law. Told him he had to leave the country, or face jail time. He argued some, so I gave him a night in jail, with a stern warning and no supper or breakfast. He agreed in the morning to leave these parts and I let him go."

Crickets chirred while the three sat in a moment of silence.

Pete, sitting in a rocker next to Jocelyn, wore a tightness in his expression, his voice the same. "That was about when a Nickel Hill fence was cut and a big bunch of our cows got out. Reckon that was a farewell get even?"

"We were lucky that one of our hired hands spotted those loose cows," Jocelyn said, wiping her forehead with the back of her hand. "Our men rounded them up and herded them back to the pasture where they belonged and repaired the fence."

"Any evidence who did it?"

"Oh, yes," Pete answered dryly. "The buggy tracks were Lafayette's. We'd seen them often enough in our own lane. One of his front wheels wobbles a trifle and it shows in the dust. His weight makes the buggy wheel prints deeper than they'd be otherwise."

Jocelyn patted her face with the hem of her apron and looked at the men. "From the direction the buggy tracks took from there, we knew then that Lafayette chose to leave the country and not go to jail. There's nothing that'd make me more relieved than if he left and never came back. Except, maybe, a long, long sentence in jail."

"That'll be next if he continues his devilment." The marshal stood up, rammed his handkerchief back in his pocket and clapped his hat on. "Promise you that."

"I hope so," Jocelyn said mostly to herself. "I surely hope so."

~

A few days before Thanksgiving at Noack's General Store, Elsa Noack approached Jocelyn, where she was placing two boxes of Lipton tea leaves, Arm & Hammer baking soda, and Morton's Salt in her basket. "I'm so glad you've come today, Jocelyn. There's something I've wanted to tell you for a while."

"What?" Jocelyn asked as she studied the shelves. She turned. "Sorry, I am listening."

"I should've told you before now, but you know how the party line is and on top of that, we've been busier than ever here in the store. Thanksgiving coming and all." She wet her lips, anticipation in her eyes. "From the first time I saw that man, Lafayette Hanley—as he claims he is, but which I doubt, I thought he looked a bit familiar."

Jocelyn froze. Her heart racing. "I've never believed him to be a Hanley, related in any way to my good friend Whit." She gripped her basket tightly. "Who do you think he really is—do you know?"

"I couldn't place him for a while and for sure I didn't know a soul named Lafayette." Elsa rushed on, hurriedly straightening a rack of women's shawls off to the side. "Right before the marshal run him out of town"—she turned to Jocelyn—"this Lafayette person came in to buy fixings for a trip on the road. Side meat, potatoes, beans. Canned tomatoes. There was a rough-looking fellow I'd never seen before with him, kind of threatening like, you know?"

"Go on, please." Jocelyn waited, hardly daring to breathe, wondering if this was the 'help' Lafayette bragged was coming to aid him in his efforts to take their ranch.

Elsa nodded. "Anyhow, I'd swear I overheard this new, rough fellow call him Scott. Not Lafayette, or Hanley. Scott." She hesitated a second, her mouth twisted in thought. "I never saw much of Matilda and Emmett Scott's children. Most of them were grown and gone when my husband"—she nodded to where Mr. Noack was busily waiting on two or three customers at once—"and I came here to Skiddy and bought our store." Her eyebrows raised, giving Jocelyn a questioning gaze.

"Scott?" She stared at Elsa, her mouth wide open in

shock. "That's the name of the family that sold Nickel Hill to Whit Hanley's father." Her skin crawled. *Could this leach who called himself 'Lafayette Hanley' be a member of the Scott family? Posing as a Hanley to rob Nickel Hill away from Pete and me?*

"I think he probably resembles his pa, Emmett, and that's why I thought he looked familiar. In looks only, Emmett was a good man, kind and gentle. So was his wife, Matilda, a nice person." She hesitated, seeming to gather her thoughts, and continued. "One of the sons was at Mrs. Scott's for a visit one time, and he was with her when she came into the store. I think that he's the one I saw recently. He's that son. His name would be Dillard, Dillard Scott."

Jocelyn stood with a hand over her mouth, her heart thudding, feeling deeply relieved to know who the scoundrel giving them so much trouble, really was.

"What are you going to do, you and Pete, Jocelyn?"

"Heaven knows, I don't. What I do know is that we have the only legal deed to Nickel Hill, and the ranch does not belong to this fake relative of Whit Hanley. I can also hope, now that the crook has been chased out of these parts, that we'll never see him again. Thank you ever so much for sharing this, Elsa. It's important information, and I will go see the marshal, or his wife, Deputy Cora, today before I leave for home, and I'll let them know what you've told me. It'll surely be of help if he ever bothers us again."

"Why do you suppose this Scott fellow, if it is him, was attempting this? This unbelievable charade?"

She sighed, and her palms lifted in confusion. "Because he grew up at Nickel Hill and feels he has a right to the ranch?" She gave a nod. "He would know that after his father died, and then his mother, that he and the other grown children sold the ranch. To Whitman Hanley, senior, the financier, making it no longer theirs. Mabel Goody told me about that when we first took over Nickel Hill as managers. Mrs. Scott's children split the money, according to Mabel, and took off in all directions, not the least interested in the work of the ranch or before that, helping Mrs. Scott, their own mother. What I've been thinking is that Lafayette—well, likely Dillard Scott—wants the ranch only to sell it, pocket the money for himself, leaving out others in the family."

"I think you're right, Jocelyn. Dillard Scott looks more like a lazy baker who eats most of his baking, than a rancher with a lot of work he likes to do."

Jocelyn shook her head and chuckled. "I need to be going, Elsa. Thank you so much for the information. I'm sure it will be of interest to our town marshal and possibly the county sheriff, too, if any more dealings with the scoundrel come up." She gathered her purchases at the counter, asked Elsa to add stick candy for Andy, whose face was practically pasted to the glass case. At the door, she turned back and called, "Have a happy Thanksgiving, everyone." She placed her hand on her young son's shoulder. "Tell folks Happy Thanksgiving, Andy." He chortled the words around the root-beer stick candy in his mouth, causing those in the store to laugh and wish Happy Thanksgiving in return.

Jocelyn put her basket of wrapped groceries behind the seat in the buggy, climbed up beside Andy and took up the reins, backing the large buggy out into the street. She turned toward home, thinking, *I surely do hope it will be a happy one. From now on, our family life peaceful again, as it should be.*

~

A more or less quiet and peaceful winter followed, except for too many weeks passing without a letter from Nila and John, causing Jocelyn fits of worry. Then a joyful letter from them would arrive. Taking breaks from covering the Young Turks Rebellion, glowing words revealed that they were learning to ski in Switzerland, had seen the Danube River, romantic castles, picturesque painted houses and snowy Alps in Bavaria, and much more. Jocelyn delighted in the stories and could relax, then, for a time.

She tried to forget the kaboodle with Dillard Scott, alias Lafayette Hanley but he remained a dark smudge in the back of her mind. It was little surprise, with the coming of early spring in 1908, quicker than they could track down the offender, one crooked stunt occurred after another on the ranch. A young calf was found tied to a fence so that grazing was near impossible, and it couldn't get to water and was close to dying. Jocelyn couldn't help tears over the calf, or growing horror, and anger, as gates in the far reaches of Nickel Hill Ranch were wrenched and hammered down, leaving stock to run loose, some never found. Likely stolen.

A sorrel horse that had belonged to Nickel Hill's hired hand, Asa—also known as Skeeter—had been let out of the pasture and was found wandering free on the road. A bushel basket of cow patties was dumped in the well where the family got their drinking water, the basket tossed aside.

Most of the crimes were committed unseen after dark, with hit-and-miss attempts to erase tracks. The culprit or culprits long gone by the time their dirty deed was discovered. The fading buggy tracks that were carelessly attempted to be brushed out could only be Dillard Scott's. When more cattle disappeared, horses' hoofprints showed along with buggy tracks, clear that Scott had been joined by two other riders. Thieves, a good guess being they were his brothers who intended to have a share of the take when Dillard got the ranch.

Pete was furious. "If he and his gang think these stunts will run us off this ranch, the fool really isn't using his brain. His brothers, if it's them helping him, are as big a fool as he is."

"They're not just stunts," Jocelyn said solemnly, "when you look at the terrible results."

"No, they're serious crimes, and I'm going to wring the idiot's neck when I find him, turn every one of his buddies, or brothers, over to the law for a good long spell in the county jail."

Their ranch hands, Web and Asa, did their best to keep watch on the matter, often carrying a rifle when out on the range, and the vandalism in revenge slacked off.

One day, sharing coffee in Mabel Goody's kitchen, while Andy played fetch outside with the Goody's dog, Jocelyn told Mabel how Elsa Noack at the store had cleared up who Lafayette Hanley surely was, and added, "If this Dillard Scott didn't live in these parts the last several years, I can't help but wonder how he came to know so much about the ranch. That we were the owners, not the older Whitman Hanley who bought it. That we inherited from Francina Hanley Gorham, didn't have to buy the property. He seemed to know it all, and that information must be behind his coming here and claiming the property was his, by inheritance."

Mabel pinned her arms close against her stomach and grew unnaturally quiet. She set her coffee aside. She gave Jocelyn a long look and her chin quivered when she finally spoke, tears shining in her eyes. "It's me, Jocelyn. It's all my fault." She drew a delicate hand-kerchief from under the cuff of her sleeve and wiped her eyes. "It's only recently that I realized what I'd done, not on purpose or meaning any hurt, though. I've tried to call you and apologize but the line is always busy."

"What are you talking about, Mabel? Don't cry. You can't possibly be behind all the trouble this Scott person has caused us. Now tell me, what's this about?"

Mabel chewed her lip, her face gone pale. "It's this way. Matilda Scott and her husband had a daughter and three sons. One day, quite a while back, I received a letter from the daughter, Rowena. Her mother, Matilda, had been a close friend of mine, and I was happy as a rabbit in clover to hear from her daughter. A dear young woman."

Jocelyn, lifting her shoulders, looked at her, puzzled. "Nothing wrong with that. Is there?"

"Well, yes there is." She shifted in her chair, darting glances at Jocelyn. "Rowena wanted to know how things were with her mother's old ranch. Wrote how much she, herself, missed it. She told me how the prop-erty got its name. That when her folks bought it, they only had a few coins left so named the ranch, Nickel Hill. But I already knew that from Matilda telling me. She wanted to know who lived there now. Wondered if

Mr. Hanley, who bought the property, had moved onto the ranch. Or did he sell it?" She swallowed and wiped her mouth with the hanky. "Jocelyn, I can't tell you how sorry I am, I should have told you about this right away, but I saw no harm in it. Then. What I did was answer her back, just thrilled to pieces to tell her everything that happened with you and Pete at Nickel Hill."

"Dear heaven." Jocelyn's hands covered her mouth.

"Yes. I wrote her that you came there with a herd of mules for young Whit Hanley, owner by then of the ranch. How you and Pete, after you married, became managers. I wrote her about how the young Whit was murdered, leaving the property to his mother in a will. Then, a couple years later, when Whit's mother died, you and Pete were the heirs, that Nickel Hill Ranch became yours free and clear. The inheritance from Whit's mother who thought the world of you two and had no one else to pass the ranch onto." She rested her head on the back of her chair and took a deep breath. She looked at Jocelyn, her face red with guilt. "I'm so sorry. I don't think Rowena told her ornery brothers what I'd told her, if she knew how they'd use it. Or maybe she knew, and they forced her to tell, you know, threatened to hurt her some way if she didn't."

Despite feeling sick inside, Jocelyn wanted to relieve Mabel's concern. "You didn't do anything wrong, Mabel. There was no way for you to know that those details would be used in chicanery, as it turned out. An effort to steal Nickel Hill away from us." *But why, oh why, didn't you tell me about this sooner?*

A sadness filled Mabel's face. "I expected to hear back from Rowena Scott, a thank you at the least, but no, nary a word. Hurt my feelings. Then, when this

Lafayette Hanley person, really Dillard Scott, come claiming Nickel Hill was his and seemed to know so much about you and Pete and how you came to own the property, I knew blessed well where he got his information." She looked at the wall then back at Jocelyn. "It'd been a while before I heard about all the dirty mean shenanigans he was giving you over Nickel Hill Ranch. By then, it looked like you and Pete were taking care of the matter fairly well, though."

"We are, with the help of the law. Truth is, the mean tricks and cattle stealing appear to have slacked off. We're not counting on it yet, but we like to think the crooked rascals have finally given up, facing facts. I think what you've told me is a good bit of information to pass along to add to what Marshal Hillis and the county sheriff already have. Both are doing what they can to help us." She was quiet a moment. "Pete would like to take this on himself, but he can't always be after outlaws and still work the ranch. It eats at him badly, at times— until the thievery and cruelty seems to have come to an end."

"Poor Pete, you tell him how sorry I am."

"I will, but you're not the problem. I know you'd never have said a word if you'd had any inkling how it'd be used. It's Dillard Scott and whoever has joined him in making our lives awful, never knowing what they'll do next to ruin us." She gave a heavy sigh. "I better find my boy and head for home."

SIX

Jocelyn was humming happily to herself in the attic. It had taken her an hour or two to clean and rearrange, put away the family's winter clothing and sort out those for summer. Finished, she climbed down the stairs and hurried to the kitchen. *Thank Hannah, she had leftover beef steak, baked beans, canned tomatoes, and homemade bread for dinner.* Still humming, she set the table and stirred the fire under the coffee. Holding her skirts, she hurried to the barn to tell the menfolk at work there, including Andy, that their dinner was ready.

She burst into the barn, saw Pete and young Skeeter at their chores, trimming five horses' hooves and seeing that they were newly shod. "Come on, you all, I've dinner ready, and here you are still working on these steeds and forgetting to eat. I have plenty of work of my own, you know, so come onto the house and let's get this meal over with." She looked around again at the two and Web. just coming through the wide barn door with his horse, a blaze-faced dark bay, from where he'd been out doctoring cattle's screwworms.

"Where's Andy?" Jocelyn asked, chin lifted, hands on her hips.

Pete said, without looking up from trimming a horse's hoof, "He's with you, isn't he?"

"No, he isn't. I haven't seen him all morning. He came here to the barn, wanting to be with you men and the horses."

"Damn." Pete stood up, stretching his back. "Wonder where he's got himself off to?' He looked around for a moment. "He said he wanted to get the mail for you and see if there wasn't that thingamajig, the box kite, we helped him send away for. When he didn't come back, I just figured he was with you. That his box kite must've come, he had it together and flying."

"There's no mail at the house, and I haven't laid eyes on Andy since he came up here to the barn. Pete, something must have happened to him. We all have to stop what we're doing and start looking for him right now. I'll check the outbuildings." She stopped. "No. Maybe he's up in the loft, played a while, and fell asleep. Andy." She put her hands around her mouth, looking up at the loft. "Andy, if you're up there, come down. Dinner's ready." Empty silence followed, and panic built inside Jocelyn. Tears started in her eyes and she swept them away with the back of her hand.

She quickly climbed to the loft to be sure. Stumbled through the hay. Climbing back down, she turned to face the men. "He's not up there."

They looked at her with sympathy and alarm. Web took the worm treatment salve he'd been using and shoved it in place on a shelf. He led his horse into a stall then proceeded to search the stanchions in the cow milking part of the barn. Skeeter began to look in every feed bin and corner. Putting his nippers and hoof knife away quickly, Pete briefly held Jocelyn in his arms and wiped her tears. "Everything is going to be alright," he told her, his own voice husky with concern. He hurried outside, Jocelyn following. A search began in every outbuilding on the property.

Jocelyn, rushing to the chicken house, stopping on the way at the pig pens, checked both. She halted to call again, and again. Her throat ached when he didn't answer. "Andy," she shouted wildly. "If you've done something you shouldn't and are hiding, you come here to me this second. Now."

Nothing.

Every foot of the ranch buildings and pastures were searched through and through. Jocelyn returned to the house, thinking she might have missed him there. From room to room, she looked and called his name. It was plain that he wasn't there, either. She set the coffee off the stove with a shaking hand. Sat in a chair, trying to clear the terrible fear in her mind and think straight. Andy had been hurrying to the mailbox out at the road for days now, hoping his box kite had arrived. He'd gone to look for mail again today. She jerked to her feet and stumbled from the house, hurrying in that direction. When she arrived at the end of the lane, a few feet away from the mailbox, she turned to ice at what she saw.

A flurry of odd boot tracks in the dust showed what must have been a furious scuffle. Some of the boot tracks were smaller than a man's—Andy's. Fear gripped her. Someone had been there on horseback. Hoofprints churned this way and then that, and back to the road leaving, heading into the less populated distance. He had to have called out for help unless a hand was clamped over his mouth. She stumbled to a clump of dusty weeds and shaking all over, picked up Andy's hat. Crushing it in her arms, she began to wail from the bottom of her soul. "Andyeeee!" Over and over until Pete came to clutch her tight in his arms. She pointed to the revealing tracks, choking the words out as she sobbed. "He's gone, Pete. They-they've taken our son."

"Go to the house, sweetheart, and call the town marshal and the county sheriff. Tell them what's happened. That our son's come up missing and from signs we've found, that he's been taken by somebody on horseback."

In the house, Jocelyn's hand shook so hard she could hardly take the earpiece from its hook. She cranked the phone a turn for the telephone office and listened to the buzz at the other end.

"C-central, give me the-the Skiddy m-marshal's office, and hurry, please. My-my son has been-been kidnapped. After I've talked to Marshal Hillis, I-I want t-to call the county sheriff's office in Council Grove."

The soft clicks of neighbors taking down the earpiece on their phones to listen in on her call reverberated in her ear over and over. Half the county eavesdropping.

Instead of the displeasure she usually felt, having all and sundry listen in to her calls, she was washed with relief and thankfulness and spoke quickly. "All of you listening in, this is Jocelyn Pladson, as you likely know. Someone has-has kidnapped our boy, Andy."

The sound of gasps and cries of sympathy filled her ear. She swallowed the fear threatening to choke her. "Would you please help us find him? Our son was taken by somebody on a horse. Andy is seven years old, medium tall for a boy, his hair the color of wheat like his father. He's without the hat he wears constantly, I found that where he was taken from, out by our mailbox. Andy is wearing a blue shirt and brown pants. Black boots. Please keep an eye out for any sign of him. We need you, please, help us—"

She stepped back a minute. Marshal Hillis was on the line trying to talk to her. She swallowed, licked her lips, and then poured out to him what'd happened.

When she was off the phone, she realized that she hadn't looked in the mailbox while she was there. Maybe Andy's precious box kite had come. Did he even have a chance to look before he was grabbed, probably beaten, and taken? Weeping and sick with worry, she fled to the mailbox, quivering inside as she opened it. With a stab of shock, she saw nothing inside except a dirtied scrap of paper. Her hand trembled as she picked it up and read the hurried scrawl.

> *I got your boy. You ever want to see him again? Next time I come to talk, we do business. OR ELSE.*

Jocelyn slumped to the ground, unable to stand, the vile note wadded in her hand. With effort, moments later, she climbed back to her feet taking deep breaths. She straightened her shoulders.

"Damn you, Dillard Scott. I know you did this even if you didn't sign this rotten note. Damn you to hell, burn in fire!" She said it with an animalistic growl in her throat, tears flowing from her eyes. Her heart hardened, and she continued cursing him all the way back to the house, swiping the tears from her face. He would pay, he would pay for this—taking her son. Pay dearly. And if he hurt her son at all—*at all*, she couldn't think of punishment fit enough.

From the moment of her phone calls, a search for Andy spread. Marshal Hillis and Deputy Cora, his wife, first checked where Dillard Scott had been staying and found little of anything that might help. People were searching high and low on their own properties on horseback. Many others in their wagons or buggies, some on foot, searched every lane and road for Andy, for some helpful sign of him, of where he might be.

Jocelyn desperately wanted to be searching, too, but was ordered by Pete to be safe at home, waiting by the phone for news of finding him. Waiting, hour after hour, was the hardest thing she'd done in her life. Women friends who came to sit with her and wait, finally gave up trying to carry on a conversation. Instead, they sat close by, one or the other holding her hand. Another made Jocelyn a cup of tea which she let sit untouched, turning cold. Her mind returned to the difficulty she'd had to be 'in the family way' to have a baby in the first place. So much time went by, so many things to try to have a child, with no luck. And then, Andy. Their precious son. Their only child. She was never 'with child' again. She got up and went to Andy's room, found his sock monkey from his babyhood and sat holding it to her heart.

Daylight ended, and the search continued into the dark, searchers carrying lanterns and lit torches. Pete, their hired men, and friends came in a few at a time for fresh horses and out again. Elsa Noack called to tell Jocelyn that every nook and cranny of Skiddy was being searched. Next day, Grant Sanborn called to tell her he'd heard of the kidnapping of their son and searches were being made in his direction, between the Pladson ranch and White City, on to Council Grove, and on from there and to be continued every day and night until Andy was found.

That night and half the next morning passed with Andy still missing and Jocelyn sick with worry. She paced the house all day, from window to window, seeing searchers come and go empty-handed. No one finding her boy. She hadn't slept, pain rocketed in her head from a headache.

On the second day, going out of her mind with worry, she thought she only imagined the sight of a rider approaching from the west through saddle-high tall-grass pasture, something, a boy, in front of him in the saddle. Minutes later, she saw for certain that it was Skeeter, their hired hand, with Andy. She tore out of the house and ran as fast as her feet could carry her to meet them.

"Oh my heavens, son, what have they done to you?" His shirt and pants were torn and dirty. Worse were dried streaks of blood on his clothes and his hands, the skin practically worn off his wrists. He slid off Skeeter's horse into her arms, relief filling his face.

"I'm alright, Momma," he choked out. "I'm alright now that Skeeter found me and cut me loose."

Skeeter swung from the saddle, wearing a proud smile. "He almost got away from them by himself, ma'am. That's barbed wire that did the damage to his clothes, his hands and arms. Rope burns on his wrists are from him being tied up."

Andy looked up at Jocelyn, wiped his dirt and blood-grubby face and pulled slightly away. "When they was taking me away, the outlaw's horse, a stallion, didn't like havin' me, a second rider, on his back, Momma. He bucked like all get out and threw me off. While that darn outlaw was tryin' to control his horse, I took off runnin'. I'd a' gotten away, too, if I hadn't got caught tryin' to stretch lines of barbwire to crawl through."

Skeeter agreed with a fierce frown. "Them damned men like to've ripped him apart, gettin' him out of the barbed wire. If I get a look at them, it'll be the sorriest day they ever lived."

Jocelyn was beginning to shake and bit her lips to keep from wailing. She was finally able to say, "Come back to the house with me, you two. Later, you can tell us what happened after the barbed wire trouble. You need to be fed and cleaned up." She pulled Andy's young body tight against her as they walked to the house, rubbing at tears with her other hand on the way.

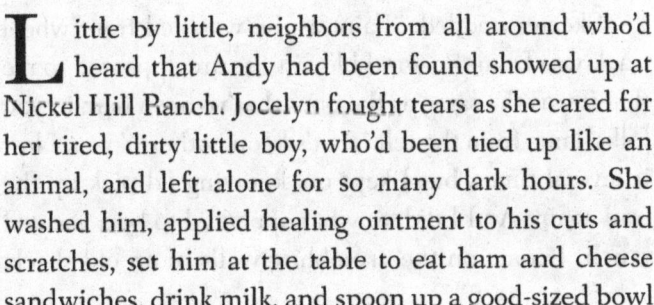

Little by little, neighbors from all around who'd heard that Andy had been found showed up at Nickel Hill Ranch. Jocelyn fought tears as she cared for her tired, dirty little boy, who'd been tied up like an animal, and left alone for so many dark hours. She washed him, applied healing ointment to his cuts and scratches, set him at the table to eat ham and cheese sandwiches, drink milk, and spoon up a good-sized bowl of chocolate pudding. Sleepy, he nearly fell off the chair when he finished. Pete carried him to bed and Jocelyn tucked him in. She stroked his hair, kissed him and tiptoed from his room. The whole story of what happened, how Andy was found, would wait until Andy and Skeeter had eaten, cleaned up, and finished their nap. Later, on the crowded porch, the group, including Marshal Hillis, told their story.

"I never come back from searching the other day because finally I'd found hoofprints that just kept going north, hard to see at times." Skeeter tilted his chair back on two legs and ruffled his fingers through his thick hair. "Not sure why, I just had a feelin' that I'd found the trail of the bugger who took our Andy. Right off"—he motioned with his arm—"they led across the Morris County border into Geary County."

"Right out of my territory," Marshal Hillis grumbled angrily. "Not that that would stop us."

Skeeter continued. "That's when I saw buggy tracks joining up with the horse hoofprints. I got off and checked the dusted-over buggy tracks for quite a piece. I could see a buggy wheel print that sorta wobbled off a bit."

"Damn," Pete said. "That would've been Dillard Scott's contraption."

Skeeter nodded. "Faint as the wobbled front wheel track was from the wind blowin', it sure appeared to me that it was the same as the ones that've been here in you folks' lane, from the fella that's been botherin' you. I lost it several times, but I kept on, knowing I'd pick up the trail again. And I did, to what appeared to be a vacated ranch. I come on the crumbling walls of an old shack, likely collapsed by a tornado and thought I heard some-one, or somethin', cryin' under that pile."

"Lord help us," someone whispered in the quiet, attentive crowd.

Jocelyn sat on a porch bench, her arm around Andy beside her. Speechless, tears filling her eyes, she nodded for Skeeter to continue.

"What did you do, Skeeter?" Pete asked from where he stood behind Jocelyn and Andy.

"I laid flat on my belly and crawled underneath the tented shambles of fallen wood and in the dim light, I saw Andy tied to the wreck of an old iron bed. I told him not to cry, I was there to take him home."

Andy spoke up, leaning forward. "I wasn't cryin' cryin'," he protested. "I was just mad as hell 'cause I couldn't get my jackknife out of my pocket and cut the damn rope keepin' me tied there."

Jocelyn bit her lip, shocked at his cussing, but not surprised considering how often he was exposed to swear words. In this situation, she decided, she'd let him go without a scolding. Until later.

Skeeter grinned. "I was tickled as the dickens to find Andy, to be able to squirm under the pile to him. I cut them ropes and when we was out, hustled him to my horse and into the saddle. Told him that we had to get back here quick as we could, give his folks ease that he was okay, find him some food. We'd find water for him to drink, a crick close by." He scratched his jaw. "I asked him if he'd been all by himself in the pile of old wood for more'n two and a half days. Did Dillard Scott, or his brothers take him there?"

Andy wiped his nose with his hand, remembering.

"All three of them was there, an' took off soon as they got me tied good to the rusty wrecked bed."

"Did they happen to say where they were going?" the marshal asked quietly.

"Nope, not really." Andy gazed at the marshal for a long moment. "But I thought maybe one or all of them might go back to Nickel Hill and our mailbox. I heard 'em talking about owners' papers to our ranch." His eyes widened in disbelief. "Claimin' to one another that Nickel Hill rightly belonged to them." He spat his next words out. "If I heard right, Momma and Papa were supposed to sign papers that'd give our ranch to them. One of the brothers of the man who kept coming here, making trouble for Momma and Papa, was to put a note in the mailbox for them to find." His lip trembled. "They was supposed to trade me back to Momma and Papa for the ranch. But I heard 'em say they'd leave me to rot right where I was if they didn't get their way." His voice shook, lowered to a whisper "And they'd say they never knew nothin' about takin' me."

Cries of sympathy and rumbles of anger rose across the porch. A single sob tore from Jocelyn's throat and she hugged Andy tightly. "Never. That will never, ever happen." She stood and not for the first time since her son had been found, hugged Skeeter. "I'll never be able to thank you enough for finding Andy. It's considerable thanks, I'll tell you that." She kissed his cheek.

The group shortly began preparing to leave. Shaking hands, sharing awed or angry comments, asking what else they might do.

To the latter, those wanting to help, Marshal Hillis announced he'd like to organize a search party immediately before Dillard Scott and his brothers found Andy gone and light out to leave the country, not get caught. He looked at Skeeter. "I'd like for you to come along, too, take us to where Andy was kept, for starters."

Skeeter looked at Pete and Jocelyn in question. "Go," they said in unison. Pete added, "I'm coming, too."

"We'll have plenty of men, Pete." The marshal's hand axed the air, his expression thoughtful. "You stay here and guard your son. Can't tell if or when they might come here to Nickel Hill and what they'll try."

Pete rubbed the back of his neck, jaws clamped for a few seconds. "Stupid fools! All right, I reckon I better."

When they'd all gone and Jocelyn and Pete were alone, Andy playing in his room, Pete stood with his arms crossed and his eyes cold. "Dillard and his brothers are crazy to think they could get away with such an idiotic scheme."

Jocelyn agreed. "No one around here is foolish enough not to recognize thieves in possession of the ranch by criminal means. That no matter what, we'd get Andy, turn the law on them, and never give up our ranch to such blind and vicious dullards."

"Amen," Pete said tightly, still looking worried. "Amen."

Jocelyn went into his arms and they held one another close for a few minutes, then went to Andy's room, to sit on his bed and watch him patiently piecing his box kite together from where he sat on the floor.

SEVEN

The posse's search for Dillard Scott and his brothers began with a trip back to the tornado-ripped shack in Geary County where Andy had been held. It was hoped that the Scott brothers had returned to check on their young prisoner and then pounding away, left a new trail to follow. Sadly, there wasn't a single sign that they'd been back at all. They'd left him by himself from the day they put him there, tied up, hungry, and frightened. It made Jocelyn sick to think of it. How she hated what they'd done to her child. At the same time, she was deeply thankful that Andy had been found before his situation worsened.

The newest hoofprints were from Asa's "Skeeter's" arrival and taking Andy home on his horse. A long, unrelenting search followed with ribbons of searchers across the prairie and towns, but it appeared that the trio had vanished for good. Folks concluded that the Scotts knew they were in for a stretch in prison if caught and they'd departed that part of the country. Until a barmaid, who had relatives in Morris County and knew about the case, spotted them in an Abilene saloon and secretly let the local law know. They were arrested and returned for trial in Morris County.

Arm in arm, Jocelyn and Pete, leaving Andy to spend the day with Mabel Goody, hurried up the steps of the Council Grove Courthouse, found their bench seats and looked at one another in hopeful expectation. Jocelyn felt practically giddy thinking this could be the end of their troubles with Dillard Scott and his brothers. That they'd pay for taking her son and leaving him miles from home, tied up in a fallen shack, probable victim in time of a hungry wolf, pack of rats, or slow death from starvation. Thank goodness, today he was with Mabel and her husband, safe for the time she and Pete had to be away.

Her hope faded a trifle when she saw that the presiding judge would not be her old friend, Judge Rawlins, whom she first met on a mule drive to Skiddy. Meeting him further times such as when he presided over the case of Herman Taggert charged for rustling cattle under his mother's cruel influence.

The defense lawyer for the Scott gang was a large self-important behaving man who paced, fiddling with his cuffs in impatience. As the trial wore on, it was clear he had no regard or sympathy for the Pladsons or their child's safety. Because Andy was found safe and basically unhurt, the Scott gang did little harm, he declared, if it was them who took him. It was only Andy's—a child's word—that it was Dillard Scott and another man who had taken him—no other witness to prove that the evil deed was the Scott brothers. Regarding the 'ransom' note that the boy's 'return would be exchanged for the Pladson ranch', there was no signature on the note to prove it was written by Dillard Scott. Or either of his brothers.

Each time, angry groans of rebuttal from those looking on in the courtroom was silenced by the judge's hard pounding of the gavel and threats to have those particular people in the courtroom removed. As the hearing wore on, Jocelyn felt sicker by the moment. As to harassment, Dillard Scott's constant visits to argue with the Pladsons was considered little of nothing, the same with his illegal trespassing and his fake deed to the ranch. There was no solid proof as to who was cutting fence and breaking down gates to allow cows to get out, some never found. Where was the proof as to who tied the young calf to the fence away from graze and water or the cow manure tossed in their well? Buggy tracks, and a child's word simply wasn't proof enough for anything.

"Strong suspicion isn't proof," the judge concluded. He gave the three Scott brothers a weak warning, then allowed them to go free. They bounced up and out, grinning widely at the Pladsons.

Jocelyn was so filled with disgust that she couldn't bear to even look at the judge or the defense attorney as they were leaving. Every moment of the hearing had been totally unfair. Wrong. She muttered to Pete, clinging tightly to his hand, "They should've been given thirty years behind bars for what they did to our son. Andy could have-have died there in that rotting tumble of a shack, if Asa-Skeeter hadn't found him in time." She swiped at an angry tear. "And they were truly guilty of all the rest, trying every trick to ruin our lives."

"I agree, sweetheart. I agree. Those grinning asses

bother us again and I'll clean their teeth with a shotgun blast."

As days passed, they did their best to put the Scott brothers from mind and resume a normal life. It wasn't easy.

~

Jocelyn enjoyed letters from Nila but the one she'd received today made her nervous, if not frightened for Nila and John as she read it aloud to Pete at the kitchen table:

> "Dear Folks,
>
>   As you can see by my envelope, John and I are in Turkey for his work covering the Young Turk Revolution—and have been for some time. Before I get to that, a few words about the good things here in this country. The Blue Mosque, built here in Istanbul between 1609 and 1616, remains as majestic and beautiful as ever. Ancient castles at every turn. Street bazaars, especially the Grand Bazaar built in 1461, and covering hundreds of streets and thousands of shops is near unbelievable and is of the biggest in the world. Visitors shopping there get easily lost without a guide. All of it has been a treat for us. Unfortunately, as you experience the good elements, you can feel the fear and unrest among the citizens almost everywhere you go, due to the Young Turks' demand for a constitutionalized government's return to the Ottoman Empire.

It seems that in 1876 Sultan Abdul Hamid suspended such and gave autocratic power to himself. Raising the ire of the many political parties in the Ottoman Empire. For example, the upper-class groups in the Ottoman Empire are Liberals who want a relaxed form of government without economic interference. The Unionists, the working class want a non-religious government. Both want the old constitution returned, but cultural differences divide them.

There is a lot more to the Revolution or 'rebellion' I should say, but it would take my whole tablet to tell you. Oh, yes, the Armenian elite, bankers, merchants, artisans, and intellectuals, living in Turkey and are Christians, are believed to have too much power. There is an undercurrent of fear that these Armenian folks will be deported if not killed. I hope that the talk remains nothing more than rumor, God willing.

Oh my, as I sit here writing to you, John has been delivered a telegram from his newspaper editor telling us to drop plans for any further stories about the Young Turk Rebellion. To leave Turkey and Armenia immediately. Word from the Consulate is that 'Kurds and irregular Turkish troops' plan to wipe out the Christian population altogether. American missionaries are feared to be in grave danger. All for now. I'll write to you again as soon as I can, from LONDON."

Jocelyn picked up her cold coffee with a shaking hand and gulped it down. She looked at Pete. "I want them home badly before something terrible happens to them. It can't be too soon for me."

Pete reached across the table. "Don't worry, Sweetheart. Nila said they'd be leaving right away for London. Where John will cover the Olympic Games for his paper. Can't be anything safer than that."

"I hope you're right."

"I am, wife, I am." She went to his outstretched arms, and he held her, talking it over until she half-way accepted his conclusion, kissed him, and turned to her daily chores.

A few days later, Jocelyn was intensely relieved when a telegram arrived from Nila saying that she and John were safe in London.

The next morning a penny postcard arrived from Rom, mailed from the Real West 101 Ranch in Oklahoma, that had her smiling and singing all morning. At noon dinner, Jocelyn shared Rom's news with Pete and Andy. "My goodness, isn't it wonderful that Rom will be in a show here in Kansas next week, at the fairgrounds in Emporia?" Hand on her throat, she read aloud.

> *"This is just an off-shoot of the big show the Millers take to the Madison Square Garden in New York and to Europe. Won't be any Indian-hunting-bison performance, but there'll be a lot of bronc busting, bulldogging, fancy roping and trick riding to watch. Hope y'all can come. Luv ya, Rom."*

She looked at Pete as she lay the postcard aside. "Let's do this, let's go, Pete. I miss Rom and would love to see him perform, would like this chance to visit with him, find out how he's faring. Can we, please, do something for pure pleasure for a change?"

Despite swearing to do otherwise, there wasn't a day that she hadn't worried the Scott brothers, since allowed to go free, would return to give them more insane trouble. When nothing such happened, she'd come to believe it possible that the fools had come to realize how lucky they were to escape prison, had turned to other doings, hopefully far from Nickel Hill Ranch. Then there was Nila and John to worry about, where they were, on the other side of the world. But London was surely a safer place to be than Turkey.

"Yep, we'll go." He saluted her with a lift of his coffee cup. "We already promised Andy and Rom, if you remember. Web and Skeeter can take care of things here the five or six days we're gone—it'll take near a couple days to get down there and the same coming back. We can be glad it's closer than Oklahoma. Sure enough, let's do it." He put his cup down and with a big smile, left his chair, pulled her into his arms, and plastered her face with kisses. She clung to him kissing him back, chuckling between kisses.

～

At the Emporia Fairgrounds, Jocelyn, Pete, and Andy hurried through the farm exhibits, food booths, merry-go-rounds plus other rides, and dozens of trinket salesmen, to the rodeo grounds. They sat in excitement, waiting for their first glimpse of Rom. Pete explained that Rom would be busy preparing for the events he'd take part in, not to worry. Sure enough, a short while later, a parade of colorfully dressed riders in single file entered the grounds and there was Rom, on a magnificent black horse with white blaze and socks. Andy jumped to his feet, yelling and clapping. "There's Rom. There's my brother."

Rom must have heard because his glance lifted to where they sat in the bleachers and he upped his chin with a smile. Andy and Jocelyn waved, Pete just grunted and laughed with an expression of deep pride.

"Yep, there's your brother," he agreed with Andy. "And on a mighty fine horse that must belong to the 101 ranch folks."

The exciting events showing off the "Real West" began in high-powered showmanship with a steer roping contest. Jocelyn's mind went back to when Pete regularly rode in contests like today. Before they were married. She'd gone to one such in Skiddy with Tarsy Webber and her husband and she was surprised to recognize Pete in the arena riding a bucking bronc. It'd been a ten-year gap since Pete and she were youngsters, friends from neighboring farms. Pete was the first boy, and it shocked her, who didn't make fun of her cleft mouth. That was before surgery that changed her face for the better, for good. They met again that day at the rodeo and were courting from that moment. Much in love, they married and started life together, at that time, as just managers of Nickel Hill Ranch.

"I remember your friend, Red Miller, teaching Rom how to rope," Jocelyn said to Pete, when Rom was riding hard, rope swinging, after a galloping long-horn steer. The rope's loop settled over the steer's horns, Rom yanked it tight with his horse's backing help, then he scrambled down, grabbed the steer by the horns, brought it to the ground on its side and whipped a leather string around its hind feet, leaving it helpless. When Rom stood, hands in the air with accomplishment, Andy and Pete whooped at the top of their lungs and Jocelyn, clapping, nearly burst with pride and joy.

Later, as the roping and riding events continued, her thoughts were interrupted by Andy shaking her arm and pointing. "It's Rom!" he yelled. "Lookit him on that leapin' twistin' horse. Ma, watch." Andy leaned toward the action in the arena. "He ain't been throwed yet. He's stayin' right on. Yes, he is. Yes—uh, no. There he goes into the dust. That blamed horse bucked him off."

"I just hope Rom isn't hurt." She brushed her hair back, her glance intent on Rom getting to his feet and brushing himself off. He limped a little at first, then walked with no limp at all. She clasped her hands together, satisfied.

"He's not hurt at all, Momma. Look at him." Andy smiled and gave a deep sigh. "See, he's wavin' at us. Wave, Momma." He lifted his hand, whipping the air.

"Yes, he is. Truth to tell, he's waving at the whole crowd, and quite a few of the crowd are clapping for his good effort."

Jocelyn's senses heightened as two young women, each on a white-ish gray horse trotted side by side into the arena. Keeping even with each other, the girls urged their mounts faster and faster around the inside of the arena, until in full gallop they stood in their saddle holding hands as their mounts sped along. The crowd roared with excitement, Jocelyn jumped up and down until she was near breathless. She looked down at Andy, then over at Pete. "Women, young women, look at them, you two. So strong and brave. Women."

"Cowgirls," Pete said. "101 performer, Lucille Mulhall was the first to be called that, and it has kinda stuck. I think it was Will Rogers who wrote in his newspaper column that "from the time she was a little girl she could rope and tie a steer fast as any man.""

"We'd be so lucky if Lucille Mulhall was here today." Jocelyn shook her head in disappointment and sat down.

"If she was, we'd have seen her by now. She's one of the best and is likely where the main 101 Real West Ranch Show is performing."

"She's in New York, but someday we might get to see her in Oklahoma, on the 101 Ranch."

"Yup."

A half mile horse race was next, with people on their feet, yelling encouragement and cheering loudly. Jocelyn held tight to Andy with one hand and Pete with the other. Rom, on the beautiful black horse, was the third rider back, coming hard, dust filling the air as the horses pounded the track. Rom and his mount pulled ahead of the second horse and rider, then the first. Jocelyn was clapping until her hands stung.

Pete shouted, "Go, son! Go." Andy was still as stone with awe, and then he was yelling and waving his fist. "Rom, you're winning, you're the fastest and the bestest ever. Ever." Jocelyn couldn't stand any longer, sat down hard, a hand over her mouth as Rom and his horse crossed the finish line, winning by his horse's blaze. This time the whole crowd was cheering for him, for Rom. For the beautiful horse.

The show continued with clever trick roping by a young man who was taught, according to the announcer, by Oklahoman Will Rogers Junior himself.

For another hour or so, the contests continued, Jocelyn, Pete, and Andy on their feet half the time, enjoying the rodeo to the ultimate.

The last event was "bulldogging" which they remembered earned that title from "the dusky demon, Bill Pickett' who, by twisting the steer's head by its horns and biting hard on the steer's lip, brought it down. Something that he'd seen a bulldog do when he was a boy—that worked when he tried it.

The arena was quickly cleared after the bulldogging event. A band entered and played *God Bless America*, bringing the whole crowd to their feet and singing along.

Jocelyn started toward Rom when they finally saw him approaching, but Andy got there first. The three of them gathered around him and all began to talk at once. Pete clapping his shoulder, Andy dancing up and down and praising him for winning the race against so many others. Jocelyn aglow with how much she'd enjoyed the show. "Especially you, Rom, and those brave young women and their trick riding."

Rom grinned from ear to ear. "Thanks. The girls are great, for sure." After several minutes of excited chatter, his attention was caught by a group drawing close and he nodded toward them. "These folks are my friends and their parents. I'd like you to meet them." He motioned for two young men and two older couples to join them. "The smart-aleck there, the short, dark-haired guy making faces, is Earl Phipps. Full of the devil and a darn good bronc buster and bull-rider."

Earl hooked an arm with each parent and led them forward. "Mr. Pladson, Mrs. Pladson, this is my ma, Althea or you can call her Allie. Allie Phipps."

The short, plump woman in an attractive navy dress with a white collar and navy straw hat decked with clusters of white flowers smiled and came to take Jocelyn's hand. Saying somewhat shyly, "So glad to meet you, Mrs. Pladson."

"Very happy to meet you, too, Allie. This is my husband, Pete." Allie smiled and nodded.

"And this is my pa." Earl looked up at him with a fake frown. "I had a hard time getting him off the farm to come here, but you liked the show, didn't you, Pa? Oh, yeah, his name is Marcus. Or Mr. Phipps, whatever you want to call him."

The tall, good-looking, weather-beaten farmer removed his wide-brimmed straw hat and shook Pete's hand, then Jocelyn's. "My pleasure to meet you folks. And watchin' the show today is the best time I've had in years."

"For me, too," Pete said, chuckling.

Mr. Phipps's expression grew serious. "I'm guessin' you know, though, that nobody can just ride away from their farm or ranch. It don't run itself. There's always somethin' needin' lookin' after. I'm lucky a neighbor fella' agreed to do for me 'til I'm home again."

"Where you from?" Pete asked.

"Got a farm near Reading, not a far piece from here."

"Wish we hadn't had to come so far. Our ranch is up north of Council Grove, not far from the Morris County—Geary County line."

The Phipps stepped back to give the other family space. Rom slapped the shoulder of a young, rangy, carrot-haired cowboy whose Stetson hung from his hand. "This is one of my good buddies, Denny Ritter, from Oklahoma. One of the best horsemen around, his specialty ridin' and ropin'. His grandpa is a friend of Will Rogers. You probably heard the announcer say that Will Rogers taught this fella how to do fancy trick ropin'." He nodded. "You introduce your folks, Denny."

He opened his mouth to do that, saw his mother on the move toward Jocelyn and Pete. With hands in the air, grinning at her, he stopped.

"No need. We can do that ourselves." The pretty, slender lady in a pale green shirtwaist and skirt, carrot-colored hair like her son Denny's, strode forward with a good-natured chuckle. "I'm Erna Ritter. Glad to meet y'all." She grabbed both of Jocelyn's hands. "We sure like your son, Rom. A good one, he is." She released Jocelyn and turned to smile and shake Pete's hand, saying to Pete, with a nod behind her, "The fella hot on my trail is my dear husband." She gave a hearty laugh at herself.

The men shook hands. Denny's father, a sandy-haired, well-dressed gentleman, said, "I'm Dr. Denby Ritter. And I agree with my wife, Erna, these three young men are as fine as you'll see anywhere. And—"

He started to say more, but Mrs. Ritter interrupted, "Now, Denby, we have lots of time to visit." She spoke in a cheery voice, eyes shining, "We're going to have our picnic lunch over to Soden's Grove, where the mill is? We'd love it if you folks, Jocelyn, Pete, and your boys, would join us. How about it?"

Jocelyn had mixed feelings. She was disappointed not to have Rom to themselves for the short time they'd have, but she was also eager to know more about these two young men he'd chosen as yokefellows. She looked at Pete. He gave an almost imperceptible nod.

"Yes," she said with a big smile. "We're most happy to come. We'll be right along. It's on the other side of Emporia. We should be there in no time." She caught Andy's shoulder. "Come along so that we can go to the picnic area, son." She nodded to the others as they split up, hurrying to where their team and wagon or buggy waited.

"Wait a minute," Rom called. "I want to ride over with you, Ma, Pa. I'm leavin' my horse here with the other 101 stock. Everything will be heading back to Oklahoma before the day is over."

"If that don't beat all." Jocelyn beamed happily. "He wants to be with us, even for the short ride."

"I knew he would," Andy bragged. "I told him I'd never come to one of his shows again if he didn't."

"Oh, Andy, you didn't. That wasn't nice."

"I know. I told him I was just jokin'. Rom said it was what he was plannin' anyway."

"Praise Hannah for that." She wiped perspiration from her forehead, anxious for the shade at Soden's Grove and filled with curiosity about how things would go with these new people they'd just met. "Now I want you to behave the rest of the day, Andy."

If he'd heard her, she couldn't tell.

EIGHT

Jocelyn had heard from friends about Soden's Mill and Bridge, on the southern edge of Emporia, many times. Pete also knew about the old furniture mill and the newer flour mill located there on the Cottonwood River and the wonderful park where Chautauqua was held. Chautauqua being wholesome entertainment including such as William Jennings Bryan, magnetic speaker and presently running for President. Preachers, showmen, musicians, and more brought culture and entertainment, attracting huge crowds who stayed for the usual three or four days. At night camping in tents among the trees. According to Mabel Goody, Teddy Roosevelt had claimed that Chautauqua "is the most American thing in America today." Jocelyn was sure she'd enjoy Chautauqua sometime, but for now, the 101 Ranch Real West Show at the fairgrounds and picnicking here in this beautiful grove was aplenty. This was pleasurable, such a relief after the incident of Andy being kidnapped. She shook her head, not wanting her thoughts to go deeper in that direction.

"Over there," Rom was saying, pointing to where the Ritters had parked their horse and buggy, and the Phipps in their wagon were drawing up beside them into the shade of a cluster of trees. Pete followed suit into the welcoming shade. A wide space of grass was found, blankets were spread, and food baskets were hustled there from buggy or wagon.

Jocelyn couldn't help a tinge of pride as she lifted her dishes from their basket, glad she'd saved her best foods, a whole sliced ham, two loaves of fresh bread and butter, three dozen lemon sugar cookies and a quart of applesauce, for today. Rom in mind at the time, but now there were the other families. She felt her pride slide a trifle when Allie Phipps put down fried chicken in a dishtowel-lined basket, a platter of deviled eggs and a chocolate cake. In turn, her mouth dropped open at Erna Ritter's spread of wholewheat bread and roast beef sandwiches, Boston baked beans, cress salad with radishes, and celery—stuffed with cheese creamed with milk and nuts according to gleeful Erna. Finally, a golden apricot pie and straw-berry jam puffs.

"My goodness, Erna." Little Mrs. Phipps looked crestfallen and equally amazed. "Coming such a long distance, how'd you manage to fix and bring all that wonderful food?"

Chuckling over it, Erna admitted her food dishes were prepared by the chef at the local hotel where they'd stayed. She'd given him a list of what she wanted, early in the day, and they'd picked it up on the way back to Soden's Grove from the fairgrounds. "I was told that there is a booth over by the ballpark where you can buy drinks from bottled ale to lemonade and iced tea."

Rom spoke up, "Everybody tell us what they want and us fellas can fetch the drinks."

"Good," Pete said, digging into his pocket. "I'm parched."

"I can go and help." Andy looked hopefully at Rom, then Jocelyn. Both nodded and as they left, Andy ran after the three cowboys and did his best to match them in stride.

The men stood aside, talking weather, cattle prices, and whether William Jennings Bryan would win the presidency this time—none sounding exactly in favor, while the women set out dishes and eating utensils.

The meal ready, and without a word, the women smiled at one another in a united conclusion of their own. Theirs was a feast fit for kings, and cowboys. A few minutes later, the cowboys and Andy were back with the drinks. Everyone found a place to sit, said grace at Allie's request, and filled their plates.

Conversation was sparse at first, but they did justice to the delicious picnic dinner. But Jocelyn noticed that Dr. Ritter off and on stared at her and Pete, then Andy. She smiled in question at him, but he just pursed his lips, his eyebrows furrowed then released. He wanted to say something, she was sure, and yet whatever he had on his mind, he wasn't prepared to share.

Earl Phipps's father, having grown up in the area, proceeded to entertain the group with facts about the city of Emporia, situated between the Neosho and Cottonwood Rivers and founded in 1857. Timber was ample along both rivers and a large sawmill and grist-mill with machinery attached were promptly built. "It was a trifle later, in 1860, that the Soden Flour Mill was added here at the grove," he told them. "Maybe you folks would like to take a walk and see the mills and the dam?"

Heads eagerly nodded in agreement around the circle of listeners.

He continued. "During the Civil War, Emporia was one of the towns listed in Confederate George Sterling's plans for destruction. And it would have been sacked and burned if it hadn't been for eastern Kansas' folks' quick rebellion against the invasion."

All heads turned toward Emporia, wondering, projecting, looking pleased.

Earl Phipps looked proudly at his father, then his friends, Rom and Denny. "Go ahead, Pa, tell us more."

"I suppose I can, a bit more. Emporia became a place for soldiers campaigning against the bush-whackers and Indians before and during the war. The county at the time was named Breckenridge, for former Vice President Breckenridge, a high-ranking officer in the Confederate army who'd become a secessionist. On the other hand, the legislature was patriotic and anti-slavery. They renamed the county Lyon to honor Union General Nathaniel Lyon who lost his life in the Battle of Wilson's Creek the previous August." He was silent a moment, removing his hat and scratching his head. "I lost an older cousin in that battle." He stared down at his hands and his hat, then into the distance. "He was a fine feller. The whole family had a hard time getting over losing him."

A few moments of silence followed, then Jocelyn spoke up, "We're sorry about that happening to you and your family, Mr. Phipps."

He shrugged. "It's happened to so many in those cussed wars, I hope there ain't ever another one."

"Don't we all." Dr. Ritter shook his head. "But I doubt we can count on it."

His wife, Erna, wore a hopeful smile. "Can we please change the subject, just for today and the good time we've all been having?"

Phipps grinned. "I reckon we can. If your ears aren't tired yet, there's one more important thing about Emporia I got to tell you. The *Emporia Gazette* newspaper was founded in 1890 by a fella named J.R. Graham, but five years later, a young fella, Willian Allen White, borrowed the money to buy the newspaper. He's pretty blunt in the editorials he writes in support of regular small-town values, and he's quite a bit reprinted in national newspapers and magazines. In these past thirteen years, he's become the friend of presidents. His importance is growing every day, and he's becoming known as one of the greatest journalists we'll ever see. An' I don't doubt it one bit that he will be." He sat back, wiping the sweat from his forehead. "Alright, cowboys, what can you tell us about your adventures with the famous 101 Real West Show outfit?"

"I know!" Andy stood. "Rom told us a whole bunch. I can tell ya'." He bounced on his toes, burst into laughter, doubled up, and fought for control.

"What on earth are you laughing so hard about, Andy? What have those young men told you?"

He stumbled over to Jocelyn still holding his stomach but the laughter easing a bit. "Turtle races, that's what they been doing, just like horse races, only a lot slower." Andy wiped tears of laughter from his face and turned to Rom. "That's right, isn't it?"

"It's a fact." Rom grinned. He sat up from resting on his elbows on the ground and removed a blade of grass from his mouth. "Me and my friends here caught some box turtles, terrapins some people call 'em. We set up a race and other fellas got interested and started making bets on which turtle would win. The boss caught us at it and we thought we were in trouble. Might get fired and sent home. But no, boss liked the idea and said he'd like to try that on a bigger scale for 101 Ranch entertainment someday. They already have buffalo, elephants, a bear that likes to drink soda pop. Why not terrapin derbies?"

"Turtle races." Andy corrected.

Rom pulled him to the ground beside him, ruffled his hair, and continued. "101 ranch has everything, not just raising cattle and rodeo shows. If you've seen a picture of a castle, you'll sort of know what Mrs. Molly Miller's house looks like. It's beautiful and is known as the White House. Several stories high with big rooms for big men. No spurs or manure allowed inside, though."

Andy bent over and burst into laughter again. "No manure, no spurs."

"Will you please stop that, Andy? Get a hold of yourself now, please." Jocelyn had to control her own grin and noticed that the doctor was smiling at Andy. Looking at him intently. He likely knew that Rom wasn't theirs by birth and had come to live with them when he was a boy. Rom could have shared that information with Dr. Ritter's son, Denny. Possibly Ritter wondered if Andy was theirs or a child taken in. She wanted to laugh proudly at that. *He was definitely their own.*

The three young cowboys finished eating and decided to go look at the dam by the flour mill.

Andy's smile was radiant as he again walked off, one of them.

The women quickly gathered up dishes, wiping them clean and returning them to empty baskets, discussing the possibility of washing the plates and utensils over at the dam. They joined the men and told them where they were going. Before they could leave, Dr. Ritter eyed Jocelyn carefully, then Pete. "I didn't want to say anything about it in your younger son's presence. I'd heard that he was kidnapped by a bunch of outlaws, and to your good luck, he was found." His brow wrinkled. "If you don't mind my asking, but being a doctor, I wonder how it affected him? He seems fine."

This was the last thing Jocelyn wanted to talk about, but she took a breath and answered. "He had nightmares several nights after he was home again, and stayed close to either me or Pete for quite a while. He's being more his self every day."

"The kidnappers, they got heavy sentences in jail for that, I assume?" Everyone had grown quiet, listening.

Pete and Jocelyn looked at one another. Jocelyn felt too sick to say another word. Pete stiffened, a bitter frown on his face. "No, they were not sentenced to prison. They were let go."

The doctor gasped. "Not really? For kidnapping, they were found innocent?"

"The fool judge decided that because Andy was basically unhurt, was too young to be a qualified witness about the men who'd taken him, and there was no signature on the 'ransom note' there wasn't enough proof to keep them."

Allie had her hand to her mouth, tears on her

cheeks, Erna, anger flashing in her eyes, looked at Jocelyn in sympathy. "Enough. Denny"—she glared at her husband—"why'd you have to bring this up? Can't you see talking about this is painful to Jocelyn and Pete? Now let's change the subject, damn it."

Jocelyn was surprised at Erna's language and clamped her lips to halt a smile.

Denny came to Jocelyn, grasped her arms, and apologized. "Sorry about that. I hadn't heard that the kidnappers were released to go free, or I'd kept my mouth shut. What I had in mind was to celebrate with you that they'd be serving long terms behind bars." He turned to Pete. "You can hit me if you want." He stuck out his chin, bringing quiet laughter to the group.

"C'mon." Pete put his arm around Jocelyn's waist and motioned to the other men. "Let's help the ladies finish up whatever they have to do and take a walk around the park."

Jocelyn lifted on her toes to kiss his cheek. "Thanks. I want to see it all, the dam, the mills, everything." *And catch up with the boys and make sure Andy is staying with them and is alright.*

They headed first to the dam, where the river water rushed over the dam and seemed to cool the air. Jocelyn pointed. "There they are, Rom and his friends, and Andy. Down watching a group of other young fellows fishing in the river."

Mr. Phipps, Earl's father, put his hands around his mouth and yelled. "Catching anything?"

Heads down below turned and nodded. Earl shouted back, "These fellas sure are. Catfish long as your arm, fist to shoulder. Some crappie and bass."

"Wish we'd brought fishing poles." Pete shrugged.

"Maybe next time. If we can get away to come any time soon." They began to move away toward the path down to the river.

"It's a really far trip from home here to Emporia." Jocelyn waved a hand to the north. "Takes us several days, coming and going. Almost too long to leave all the work to our two ranch hands."

Erna's face clouded. "You're not going to leave for home yet today, are you? You surely don't drive at night, in the dark with a lantern. Do you camp, have a tent?"

Jocelyn laughed. "No, we don't travel in the dark or camp in a tent."

"You're staying here in Emporia at the hotel."

"No, ma'am. We'll leave before evening, not travel far and spend the night with folks we've gotten acquainted with." She went on to explain. "We've lived in the Skiddy area for years now and made friends with folks in town, in the country around us, and through a livery business I used to have. Some have friends or a relative that live not too far off the main roads to get here. They put us up for the night. We do the same at our ranch for folks heading north, to Junction City or Manhattan, for example. It's helpful for everybody. On this trip, when we get as far as Council Grove, we'll stay in the local hotel."

"Early pioneers certainly traveled that way." Erna looked satisfied. "Being put up for the night when they reach somebody's cabin. Sleeping on the floor, mostly."

Allie spoke slowly. "I suppose if you know them well, that'd be alright." She crossed her plump arms then uncrossed them, tilted her head, brushing away a tendril of hair from her face. "I'd not be sure to trust somebody otherwise. They could be outlaws, robbers, maybe."

"Pete and I have learned to take a pretty reliable measure of people. Outlaws, grafters, and the like are pretty easy to tell from decent, honest people."

A short while later, they'd caught up with the men, who were talking fishing with the bunch of young men at the river. The three 101 Real West Show cowboys were preparing to leave.

Jocelyn clutched at Rom's arm. "You're not going already, son?"

"Yeah, Ma, have to get back to the fairgrounds and help get ready for the next trip from here."

Her shoulders dropped and then hitched up again. "Of course, you need to travel on with your group. We'll take you back to the fairgrounds." She bit her lip. "I just wish we'd had more time to visit. Maybe next time. We're so proud of you, Rom. Winning the race like you did and doing well in the other competitions."

He kissed her cheek. "I'm durn glad y'all got to be here, and I'll be coming home again when I can for visits. An' you don't have to take me back to the fairgrounds, Ma. A couple other performers from the show are here with their wagon and we're ridin' back with them."

Jocelyn looked up to where he pointed. Above them, two pretty girls waited with their wagon and team. They waved. Rom waved back, then reached over and ruffled Andy's hair. "This one is sure growin' up fast. I miss him. We had us one fine time today, didn't we, brother?"

"The best." Andy stood in a wide stance, fists on

hips, and his elbows wide. Just like Rom. "We damn sure did."

"Andy!" Jocelyn gasped, hand over her mouth. "You're not to talk like that."

He grinned at her. "Sorry, Ma."

Rom's eyes glistened with humor, and his tongue bulged his cheek to stop his laugh. He gave Andy a stern look, and he caught his shoulder. "Cowboys don't ever swear in front of ladies, they really don't. Now you remember that."

Jocelyn gave Rom a last hard hug. "Don't know what I'm going to do with you two, sometimes, but I wouldn't trade you for all the gold in a Denver bank."

~

Jocelyn wanted to see Soden's Flour Mill with the others now making their way up the steps and inside. She hesitated, having heard that grit dust from the mill machinery could be explosive. She mentally chided herself. Naturally, the workers would know that and take every precaution. No lamps, candles, or pipe smokers. She hurried to catch up with Pete and Andy, waiting for her at the door.

Inside, they followed the others down steps to a lower level. "Down here is where the wheat seed is separated from the chaff and washed," Pete said. "If the wheat seed are going to be flour, it is has to be cleaned. Sticks, rocks or any other foreign matter removed before it is tempered."

Still downstairs, they watched water added to the wheat grain, then sent to a shaking sifter which made

Andy laugh. "It's like your flour sifter, Ma, but a lot bigger and throwing water."

"Somewhat like my flour sifter." She put her hand on his shoulder to stop him from violently shaking his head, mimicking the vibrating screen.

"What does *temper* mean? It can't mean wheat seed gets mad."

"No, it doesn't, son," Pete answered Andy. "It means opening the kernel, removing and flattening the brown shell, or layer of bran, and breaking the endosperm into chunks."

"What's *endosperm*?" Andy's face puckered in a confused frown, his shoulders sagging.

Pete bit back a laugh. "Endosperm is the inside of a seed. Flower seeds, as well as grains, have endosperm. It contains starch, sometimes oils, and proteins. Very healthy eating for livestock and folks. Let's go up to the next floor and see the grinding."

"These huge millstones are like wheels." Jocelyn held Andy back from the machinery, raising her voice against the grinding, clacking, squealing sounds while she explained. "One on top of the other and powered by the water wheel outside, which is piped to the turbines inside, grinding the cleaned kernels of wheat between them. The millstone on the bottom is called the bed, and the top stone the runner."

They stood watching for several minutes.

"Alright, upstairs next. That's where the ground kernels are refined into fine flour, then sent back down to the main floor where it's bagged." They watched the grain moving up a curved wooden elevator—sides like those of a boat—toward the top floor. And followed up on the stairway. For a good fifteen minutes, they watched the rolling and sifting of the flour they had seen ground from wheat seed, below, until it was soft as a cloud.

Before leaving the flour mill, while downstairs again, Jocelyn purchased a fifty-pound bag of freshly ground wheat flour which Pete toted to their buggy.

Leaving the park, Andy reached over the seat and patted the bagged flour placed behind him in the storage area of the buggy. "This'll make a lot of cookies and pie, won't it, Momma?"

Jocelyn turned and brushed flour dust off his cheeks. "It sure will, son. It sure will. Bread, too."

NINE

On the way home, Jocelyn was remembering this same route from eight years ago, at that time driving a cook's wagon with a herd of mules following. A job she'd never dreamed of but learned to love, ending up at her boss's, Whit Hanley's ranch, Nickel Hill. A happy change of life meeting Pete again after a ten-year absence and marrying him. Nickel Hill Ranch eventually becoming theirs through a legal will from their friend, Whit Hanley's mother. Her mind still wandering, she shifted on the wagon seat. It seemed a century since they'd left Emporia. It would be so good to be home again. There might be word from Nila and John letting them know for sure when they were coming home. When she, Pete, and Andy could pick them up at the train station in Skiddy.

The miles continued to drag by on this hot afternoon. She swept her dampened hair back from her face, turning to look at Andy asleep on the back seat of the buggy, shirt off and feet bare. When their ranch came in sight at last, Jocelyn shared a contented look with Pete. "So glad we're here." She laid her head on his shoulder.

He reached up and patted her cheek. "Yup, no place like home."

They turned into their lane, and Jocelyn straightened, her heart beginning to pound. "What in the name of Hannah is going on here, Pete?"

"We're about to find out." His brows pulled in. "That's Marshal Hillis's horse."

"Something's happened to have the marshal in our yard talking to our men, Skeeter and Web."

As they drew closer, Jocelyn stiffened and her fingers went to her throat, her eyes widening as she took in their two cowhands' appearance. The younger one, Skeeter, sat on the ground with his head bandaged in a bloodstained rag, blue bruises on his face. Web, leaning against the corral fence, looked as bad, his arm in a sling and his face swollen with bruises, one purplish eye closed. *Surely, they hadn't done this to each other.*

Pete drew the team to a halt by the corral and hurriedly climbed down from the buggy. Jocelyn and Andy followed. Jocelyn shooed Andy to the house. "There are cookies in the cookie jar and you can go ahead and boil yourself a couple eggs and butter yourself some bread. I know you're hungry, Andy. Stop at the henhouse for the eggs. There'll be plenty." He looked reluctant for a minute, eyeing the goings on, then grinned and skedaddled. The marshal strode across the barnyard, a pair of hens fluttering out of his path, to meet Pete and Jocelyn, his face unreadable.

"What's happened here?" Pete gave the marshal a strained look. "What in Sam Hill brought you out here, were these two trying to kill one another? Doesn't look like friendly wrestling or fisticuffs to me."

"They can tell you." Fighting a grin, Marshal Hillis shrugged a shoulder at Web who'd walked carefully over to join them and Skeeter, still seated on the ground, one arm wrapped around his knees, the other hand wiping dust off his boots.

"Well?" Jocelyn did a double take at how beaten up they were.

"They came." Web waved his good arm toward the barn. "Right soon after we finished putting the last of the hay crop up. We were cleaning the barn and water troughs."

"Who came?" *Surely not the Scott gang. After all the hullabaloo over what they'd meant to do with Andy, she'd been almost sure she'd never hear from them again.*

Skeeter pulled himself up off the ground and limped over. "Them three bad 'uns that took Andy, that's been harassin' you folks to hell and back. We had a kinda mix up with 'em."

"Tried to kill us is what," Web added, his expression grim. "They'd found out somehow that you folks were gone somewhere and wouldn't be back right off. They intended take over, move onto the place lock stock and barrel while you were gone."

"They didn't." Jocelyn grasped her head in both hands in doubt, crushing her hat. "The crazy ignorant fools. They still think that they can pull off that impossible stunt?"

"Yup. Argued with us that you don't own the place, Missus Pladson, that you and Mr. Pladson never paid a penny for it."

"In a way that's partially true. We didn't *buy* Nickel

Hill. But we earned the property, had been making payments—until Mrs. Gorham, the owner, died. The ranch was awarded to us in her perfectly legal will, a dear friend who had no one else to leave the ranch to, and they know it." She was angry enough to scream.

"They argued that meant nothin' and Nickel Hill Ranch is just as much theirs as yours, or more so, since it used to be their ma and pa's."

"It may seem that way to them, fools that they are, but the facts are definitely otherwise."

Skeeter spoke again. "We told them they had their heads on crooked and brains backward and there weren't no question—Nickel Hill belongs to you folks, legal. That's when things got nasty, them tryin' to throw us off the place and make it theirs." He nodded toward Web. "Web, there got shot in the arm. I fixed it for him good as I could, but he still needs to see the doc." He lightly touched his own bandaged head. "They clipped my ear and side of my head with a bullet. They was plumb bent on killin' us and buryin' our bodies after. Claimed you folks would think we turned lazy, got a bee in our heads and took off on our horses for good. And once they got settled in here, there'd be no way you'd get the ranch back."

Jocelyn was horrified to think their rotten plan might have gone through.

"So where are they now? They got away?" Pete's expression was stony. He turned, looking toward the road, hands in the air, and back again. "Right?"

Jocelyn had a sour taste in her mouth, fists clenched, waiting to hear the worst.

"No, no, not at all." Web grinned. "We won the mix up. Theys worse off than us, from the pistol whippin' we gave 'em. We got 'em all tied up and in there." He nodded toward the barn. "Locked in the corncrib."

"What?" Jocelyn gasped, choking on a laugh. She fanned herself. "In the corncrib?"

"Tied up and maybe still unconscious." Skeeter's eyes gleamed with pride. "An' bloody."

"I'll be damned." Pete chuckled, hands on his hips. He turned. "What's next, Marshal?"

"These two sent for me." Marshal Hillis stepped forward. "I got here quick as I could, afraid somebody was gonna get killed. I found that these young fellas had matters in hand right fine. I promise you folks, this time these rotters in the corncrib are going to jail in Skiddy for a nice long stay. My deputy wife, Cora, is coming right behind me with our wagon. She'll be here 'fore long so we can haul these three no-goods to Skiddy and lock them up. You mind keeping their horses here until I decide what to do with them?"

Jocelyn could see by Pete's expression that he wasn't really pleased to put up anything having belonged to the outlaws, but he nodded that he would.

At the rattle of a wagon on the road a few minutes later, everyone turned to see Deputy Cora whipping her team and coming up the lane in a cloud of dust. Wearing men's clothing as she usually did when on a job, her coronet of cornsilk braids jammed into her tan hat, she leaped off the wagon and hurried to her husband's side. She eyed Skeeter and Web. "I figured there'd be bloodshed. Doc Ashwood is busy with a difficult delivery of a baby, but he'll be here soon as he can. Repair these young men's wounds. Is everybody alright so far?"

"Folks outside here in the barnyard are still breath-

ing, not so sure about the prisoners in the corncrib."
The marshal hid a smirk and motioned the ranch hands
to stay put, and signaled to Pete. "C'mon, let's go get
'em outta there and in the wagon. Cora"—he looked at
her—"you're riding my horse home, following me. I'll be
driving the bast—criminals in the wagon"—he looked at
the women—"myself."

Jocelyn took Cora's arm. "Thank you so much for
this, Cora. Umm-Deputy. You and the marshal both.
This should keep the Scott gang out of our hair for
good."

Cora smiled. "We'll see to it, guaranteed."

"On a charge of attempted murder and intending to
steal valuable property," the marshal called back over
his shoulder as he entered the barn.

Hands clutched together, her heart pounding,
Jocelyn waited. She caught a movement from the
corner of her eye and saw that Andy had come from the
house, or maybe had never gone inside. He came over
and she pulled him back against her, held him close.

The three Scott brothers, hands tied securely
behind them, were hauled, struggling, from the barn.
Limbs hanging limp, they looked like they'd been
dipped in blood and every inch of them pounded with
hammers. Pete had Dillard, who sagged, stumbled, and
when hauled up, sobbed like a woman. The marshal
held one brother who looked half dead, and Cora the
other who spat at her with burning hate. He twisted
and tried to grab her gun from its holster. She slapped
his hand hard, grabbed the pistol herself and gave him a
quick conk on the head. "Mind your manners!" With
Asa's help, she hauled him into the wagon. Dillard at
that same moment tried to get away. Pete yanked him

back and threw him into the wagon. The marshal added the near-unconscious brother to the human load.

"Listen, dear husband," Cora said to the marshal. "I'm riding here in the wagon with this lot of rubbish, my gun ready should they try anything. Hold up a minute. I'll tie your horse here to the wagon and were set to go." He shrugged and waited.

As the jail wagon and team took off in a rolling cloud of dust, Jocelyn gave Andy a squeeze. "I'm sorry you had to see this, son. The bloody mess these men made of one another."

Andy looked at her, his face twisted in surprise. "Shoot, Ma, how can you worry about that? After what those three did to me, not caring if I lived or died hungry, I wouldn't have missed seein' them get what they had comin' not for nothin'!"

She reconsidered. "You're right, Andy." She stroked his face, the faint scars from barbed wire healing well. "And I apologize." In the hands of the Scott brothers, there was every possibility that her son might not be alive today. "Pete"—she caught his arm—"let's take a ride into Skiddy. I'm getting low on sugar and other things I'll make note of on the way. We need to be thinking about new shoes for Andy, his feet growing like they have and school starting soon."

He grinned. "You bet. Let's do that, honey. I gotta give the team some feed and water, they've had a little rest but I may get another team. I'll wash up a bit down to the windmill tank, you and Andy be ready."

Her beloved husband had always been able to read her mind. What she really wanted to do was see the Scott brothers locked tight behind bars with her own eyes. She removed her apron and ran to the house for her handbag and the money she'd need. When she looked out the window, Pete was already hitching a fresh team of horses to their buggy with Andy's help. Pete would want to follow the marshal's wagon, be close behind if help was needed. They had to hurry.

As they neared town, they saw a dust cloud ahead swallowing the marshal and Deputy Cora's wagon, carrying the three beaten outlaw brothers in the direction of the jail.

A gathering crowd was beginning to follow the marshal's wagon when Pete and Jocelyn reached town. "Hear that," Jocelyn told Pete with a smile, "folks are asking what happened and who are the men that's all bloody and torn clothes in the back of the wagon. Cora is telling them, plain and clear, who they are and what they did and for folks to please go on about their business while they lock their prisoners in jail."

"We'll follow. Take a few minutes to see that for ourselves." Pete shook the lines over the team to move them faster.

"Yes, and then we need to buy groceries before we head home."

Pete looked at Jocelyn with a grin and patted her knee. "Sure, honey, I'll take you to the store where we can buy a few things and you can casually drop our good news about the Scott gang going to prison. No better place to do that if you want to spread news." He shook his head and laughed.

She shoved him with her shoulder. "Don't tease about this, Mr. Pladson. This is serious." It was hard to be irritated. She slipped her hand in his.

Andy stood and moved forward in the buggy to stand clinging to the back of their seat. "I'm hungry.

Can we stay in town for dinner? At the hotel, maybe? Have pie for dessert?"

Jocelyn and Pete looked at one another. "Sure can." Pete turned to look at Andy. "Our team needs the rest before we turn back home. Thanks for the plan, son."

Icing on the cake, Jocelyn was thinking, *would be if those scoundrel Scott brothers would be held behind bars for the next fifty years. Surely it would be something like that.*

TEN

In the time that followed, Jocelyn and Pete's days were made more pleasant by a string of letters from Nila letting them know what a good time she and John were having at the London World Olympics. With a regret or two—they wished they'd been there to see King Edward VII open the Olympics in April, and the many athletic teams from twenty-two nations parading behind their country's flag. Nila was also miffed that out of two thousand and eight athletes, only thirty-seven were women. Someday, hopefully soon, that had to change. Nila personally wasn't particularly athletic, but she had friends who were—swimming, running. Women's baseball teams. She intended to urge the best of them to consider entering the Olympics.

In another letter, Nila wrote how impressed they were regarding Oscar Swahn, who'd won the gold medal for 'running deer shooting' and became the oldest Olympic champion at age sixty. They were proud to see American John Taylor, a member of the medley relay team and the *first African American* to ascend the highest platform and accept the Olympic Gold Medal.

Nila added that her husband, John, was constantly busy telegraphing his entertaining stories home to his newspaper, the *Topeka Daily Tribune*.

"In between times, we're enjoying brief tours of the city," Jocelyn read aloud to Pete and Andy, and the hired men, right after breakfast. "And delicious suppers at the coziest, homey restaurants. Really popular London dishes—and we like them, too—are fish and chips, steak and kidney pie, and banger and mash, the last otherwise known back home in America as 'sausage and mashed potatoes with peas and gravy.'"

"Banger? Banger and mash?" Andy doubled over in his chair, holding his stomach and laughing. "'Taters an' peas with gravy is *banger and mash*?"

"That's enough, Andy." Jocelyn put a finger to her lips, trying not to laugh herself.

Jocelyn and Pete whooped and kissed when they received word from Attorney Grant Sanborn that a full calendared variety of trials to come, would keep the Scott brothers locked tight in jail for months. Waiting for their trial. Also, the trio were having trouble finding a lawyer to represent them, according to Grant. "We couldn't be luckier," Jocelyn said, her face against Pete's chest, then looking up and hugging him.

"About time." He grinned widely, kissed her forehead, and let her go. "Back to work."

In town one day, Jocelyn spotted Marshal Hillis talking to a group of men on the hotel porch. She caught his eye, waved, and waited as he came hustling down the porch steps. They chatted for a bit about trifling matters. Then, she braced herself and asked about the Scott brothers' reaction to being behind bars.

"Hell is what it is for me and Cora. The caged fools don't let up griping how wronged they've been."

As if they were. "I'm sorry about that part of it." She frowned, chewed her lip, and wondered if she should have kept still. She wanted those horrible men kept behind bars.

He cleared his throat, his Adam's apple bobbing. "Dillard's brothers blame him for all the trouble they're in now. From what I heard in their yelling at one another, his brothers have been living the high life in Kansas City through gambling, theft, and beating up honest businessmen for a high KC muckamuck." He scratched his jaw, a gleam in his eyes. "Might be when their trial finally comes around, they'll get them for past crimes, too. Happens often."

Jocelyn's heart drummed with elation. "I surely hope so, Marshal." She rubbed her chin in worried doubt. "I don't want them to get away with what they've done, not again. Not ever."

"Yeah, me, too. I had them all in one cell." He motioned with his hands how he'd bunched them. "That led to constant fighting. Getting close to strangling or stomping Dillard to death. An' I think they would've if I hadn't got him out of there and in another cell. They still yell threats back and forth at one another. Sometimes they throw the food Cora brings them back through the bars at her. I'm darn near about ready to hang them without a trial."

Jocelyn lifted her hands and let them fall, wishing

none of this had ever happened. "I'm sorry that all this has been put on you and Cora."

"It's our job to do." He sighed. "And could get worse. When I was movin' Dillard, he almost got away before I knocked him out cold and dragged him into the other cell an' locked it. He's the biggest whiner I've ever had to deal with, but like I said, it's my job."

"Be careful, you and Cora. I don't want anything happening to either of you because of these scoundrels."

"Thanks, Jocelyn. We'll do that."

The next day, Jocelyn had gotten Andy off to school in a neighbor's wagonload of children and was drying breakfast dishes when she saw the mail carrier's buggy pulling away from their mailbox. She put the last plate in the cupboard and hurried outside to get the mail, hoping there'd be a letter from Nila and John. The letters about the Olympics were entertaining, but she couldn't help not looking forward to definite information as to when they might be coming home to America, and the final stop in Skiddy on the train. In the most recent mail from them, they hinted that they couldn't say for sure yet, but might be home earlier than originally planned. That a photographer friend of John's at the paper might be taking John's place the final weeks of the Olympics.

Hope washed over Jocelyn when she opened the mailbox and saw the envelope with Nila's handwriting. Heading back toward the house and feeling giddy, she ripped the envelope open and began to read. The next moment she stopped dead in her tracks, her hand going to her mouth. "My goodness. Oh, my goodness!" Joy flooded her head to toe. She clasped the letter to her bosom. *A baby, a baby.* Not only would they be here in two weeks, they were coming home now, in October, because Nila was with child. Jocelyn danced in the dusty lane. The couple wanted good care for Nila and their unborn infant, until the baby arrived next April. Jocelyn lifted her apron and dried the moisture from her eyes, then ran to the cornfield, the letter flapping in her hand, and told Pete the news.

Over their midday meal of leftover snap beans, sliced tomatoes, fried chicken, gravy, and biscuits—Jocelyn, excitement unabated—continued to chatter about the matter of Nila and John's homecoming. "It's only a couple weeks and they'll be arriving in Skiddy on the train, Pete," she told him for the third or fourth time. "I want to make a trip to their house before they get here, have it ready for them. They'll be tired from the ocean trip and traveling on the train from New York. Days and nights of getting little or no sleep."

"You're thinking of that baby to come, too, I bet."

She pretended to swoon. "I am, Pete. Aren't you?"

He laughed. "Sure I am, honey. The thing is, John's property in Cloud County isn't exactly next door. I'm guessing it's near eighty-five miles north of here, for God's sake. It'd take you three days to get there, stopping now and then to feed, water, and rest the horse drawing the buggy, and all of that coming back home. That's if you have no problems along the way. I don't think so, Sweetheart. I'd take you myself, so you could do this with my help, but I gotta be here. Web and Asa can't handle the work, all the harvesting chores to be done, and the neighbors busy with their own."

"I know all that." She frowned and continued her plea. "Which is why I plan to take the train. They travel much faster than horse team and buggy, anyway. There'll be a couple small-town stops where I change trains, but that's no bother. It'll take between three or four hours at most." She made strong eye contact, her hand on Pete's arm. "Andy loves trains. I want to treat him with that, Pete, and I'll have him with me to help since it'll be a weekend and no school."

Even though the culprits who'd taken him were now locked up tight in jail, since the kidnapping it was hard to let him out of her sight. "I'll take food for us. And dust cloths and beeswax to polish furniture. Soap to wash sheets and clothespins to hang them to dry." She crossed her fingers in her skirts that there'd be a clothesline still there. "It'll be a homecoming gift to Nila and John, and I know they'll appreciate it. I sure would." She chewed her lip, hoping for him to agree. "I intend to go first thing in the morning and leave our team and buggy at the new livery stable in Skiddy. Have it waiting there when we return on the train, so I can drive us home, no bother to you having to come after us." She waited expectantly.

He nodded. "You know for sure where this place of John's is located?" He gave a long, low sigh, his eyes still doubtful. "You're taking a broom and mop on the train with you?"

She laughed, her cheeks warming in gratitude that he was giving in a little, and her intentions grew. "I know where it is. Nila told me. The little town of Hollis has a train station, the Union Pacific passes through there. The farm his grandmother left him is on the edge of town. I know what the house and outbuildings look like. The house is white with blue shutters, the barn and henhouse are red, and the outhouse is—unpainted."

She pushed up her sleeves, exuding calm and focus. "John had taken a picture to show Nila, and she showed it to me. She had to tell me the color of each building and I can see it in my mind. His grandparents home-steaded there shortly after the Civil War, in 1866 or 1867, and they lived in a dugout for some years before building the house."

Pete nodded slowly. "Like so many at that time." He stroked his chin and motioned for her to continue.

"John said that when he went to his grandmother's funeral, he left everything just as it was before she died." She smiled, wanting to assure her worrying husband. "I'm positive, for pity's sake, that I'll find a broom and mop, Pete. Before they left for Europe, I told Nila that I wanted to do this for them. She said I needn't, but I insisted on having a key to the door. Now I'm glad that I did, seeing that she's with child, and that long trip across the Atlantic an' all, getting her back to Kansas. I have to do this, Pete, I must."

He stood up and drew her into his arms in a hug. "You don't change much, do you, woman? You and your big heart always have things figured out."

She kissed his cheek. "I do try. Now I've things to do to be ready."

～

Jocelyn had a lot on her mind as their train chugged toward Hollis in Cloud County, and Andy sat with another boy his age playing clapping games like A Sailor Went to Sea, laughing as they sang the silly little song. The trip passed pleasantly enough, chatting, laughing, sharing cookies with Andy's new friend. After a while they fell quiet, with exceptions to sights on the way. At one quick stop, between trains, they hurried off the train to the station lavatory and back. In no time, it seemed, they were at the Hollis station gathering up their bags as they were unloaded, in another moment familiarizing themselves with their surroundings.

"This way, son," Jocelyn started off on the dusty road from town, a warm October wind whipping them along. They'd been walking for several minutes when a wagon came up behind them and drew to a halt alongside them.

"Where ya headed?" an older, bonneted woman with a kindly face, reins to the team in her hands, asked.

Jocelyn hesitated. She'd seen the woman waiting back at the station and had watched her hug a simply dressed, pretty young woman who'd sat only a few seats away from Jocelyn on the train. They looked friendly, nice folk. She smiled and answered. "The Riordan farm, where Mrs. Annie Riordan once lived. You likely know about it."

"I do. You're about there but pretty loaded down. If you're of a mind, I can give you and your boy a ride."

"Thanks, I know where it is and we're close enough we might as well walk."

The woman on the wagon sat there quietly for a moment, not moving. "Nobody's lived at the Riordan farm for a long time. Annie died some years back. You mind my askin' your reason for going there? It's a rundown place. Fields haven't been worked in a long time. House will be dirt thick and smelly for being closed up."

"The farm was left to my cousin's new husband."

She was anxious to keep walking and took a couple of steps. "They are on their way back from Europe and it's my plan to clean the place up," she said over her shoulder. "Have it ready for them."

The woman's head jerked back, driving forward. "You'll have a lot of work on your hands, you and the boy. I'm Mrs. Kurella, Ida Kurella, the neighbor a half mile on down the road from the Riordan place." She leaned from the wagon and held her hand down to be shaken.

"I'm Mrs. Pladson—Jocelyn." She patted her son's shoulder. "This is my boy, Andy."

"And this is my granddaughter." Mrs. Kurella nodded toward the young woman beside her. "Becky Lou. You need anything, let us know." She shook the reins, and they moved on down the road. The granddaughter leaned over the side of the wagon, looking at Andy. "Don't go in the old barn. Snakes are in there."

"Well, we've been warned, son." Jocelyn bit her lip, then gave him a smile of encouragement. "Just a short way now. Let's go have a look at what we have to do."

Andy gave the dusty road a sharp kick with the toe of his boot. "I wish people would stop treating me like a baby. "I know dam—darn well there's snakes in lotsa barns. Mostly black snakes, three or four feet long and harmless."

Jocelyn bit the inside of her cheek to keep from laughing. "You're right, son, about the black snakes in barns. No worry about them. It might be smart, though, to keep an eye out in case this barn has a different, more dangerous, type of snake."

He looked at her for a long minute, his face turning red. "I s'pose."

The small house was nearly buried in weeds and the lock so rusted the key wouldn't work. Jocelyn twisted and turned the key, trying to poke it in again and again twisting and turning, over and over until she was almost ready to use the swear words she scolded Andy for using. *They had to get inside. They had no other shelter, no place to sleep or put their things and they'd come so blamed far.* Close to desperate tears, she tried one more time. The lock clicked, she tried the door, and it opened. They were met by a musty smell of mice and things unknown in a house long unused. They left footprints on the dusty floors exploring three sparsely furnished rooms and a back porch. Outside, Jocelyn checked the sun and saw it straight up at noon. Good, she had time to wash the bedding and have it dry by bedtime. The tubs were easy to locate hanging on the back porch, as well as the washboard and a bench. *Water, she had to have water, and wood for a fire to heat it.*

At the well, bucket in hand, she found that the windmill rattled and clanked but some of the workings above her head were likely rusted and some broken and couldn't draw water.

Back in the house, she stripped the bed and shook out the sheets and comforter from the back porch, dust flying and making her sneeze. At least she and Andy could lie down on a dust-free bed, but she hoped to find a source of water. Luckily, she'd brought sandwiches and apples for their midday meal. "Let's eat quick as we can, Andy, then we'll walk to Mrs. Kurella's and ask to borrow water. We don't have a lot of time if I'm going to wash bedding and have it dry by tonight."

Andy had eaten one sandwich and picked up

another, stuffing an apple in his pocket. "Let's eat on the way, Ma."

"Good idea, Andy." She munched on her sandwich in hand, put an apple in her apron pocket, and outside, led the way to the road. "A half mile isn't far. If they'll give us water from their well, you and I can tote a tub partly filled between us. Maybe go back for a bucket or two more if needed. We'll get this cleaning done, we have to."

Chin lifted, she marched along, pride and purpose having stiffened her spine. Andy, falling behind throwing rocks at fence posts, hurriedly caught up and matched her step.

ELEVEN

I n short order, they'd reached the Kurella farm, spotting Mrs. Kurella in the barnyard. Nearby was a short, well-muscled, ruddy-faced man in overalls and worn shirt. He looked up and gave them a short wave. Helping him was a lanky, dark-haired teenage boy. Together they were busily filling large, twenty-five-gallon metal milk cans with water from their well. Jocelyn stopped and stared. From what she'd heard, milk cans this large were first made on the Isle of Guernsey and pounded into shape the same way armor of the time was made. She took a few hesitant steps forward, watching them load the cans into a wagon as she and Andy reached the activity. *Surely, they're not doing this for us, I haven't even asked. Yet.*

Mrs. Kurella stood in the shade from the barn, smiling, her hands on her hips. "Afternoon. Good to see you and the boy, Mrs. Pladson."

"Good afternoon. You're not...?"

"About to bring you milk cans of water. Sure as bells ring on Sunday, we are." She spoke with an expression of satisfaction and a wave of her hand. "After hearing about the hard work you plan, coming out of nowhere, we knew you'd likely not have water. That old windmill on the Riordan property hasn't been used for a half dozen or more years, you know. It'll take some greasing and fixing to get the gears, sucker rod and all going proper again. Our son here, Jonas, will be over there. He's like a monkey, climbing and fixing windmills."

"I don't know what to say. This is so generous of you all. Thank you, Jonas." She watched the young man toting another milk can of water to where his mother was climbing up into the wagon.

He grinned. "Ain't nothin'." He hefted it into the wagon and shoved it back with the other cans he and his father had loaded.

His mother spoke up. "Pshaw, my mother used to tell me, 'Help one person, and you've helped the neighborhood.' That's what we're doing and glad to do it." She waved a hand. "Now we got this water loaded, you and the boy get on the wagon with me here, and we'll head back to your young couple's place."

When she was seated next to Mrs. Kurella—Ida, Jocelyn eyed the brooms, mops, a basket of rags, two bars of yellow soap and the like in the back with the milk cans and Andy. She looked at Mrs. Kurella and told her, "I brought a few cleaning things with me from home. I hadn't looked but I expect to find a broom and mop on the back porch. Thank you, though, for bringing yours."

Her new friend laughed. "Years-old soap, broom, and mop might be like new. But in case not, I'm bringing what we need."

We? She was going to help clean up the place, too?

At the sound of a horse's hooves clopping up close behind them, Jocelyn turned and saw the Kurella's son, Jonas, following, a bag hanging from the saddle-horn, likely holding tools and oil for the windmill. Jonas on the horse, and Andy hanging off the side of the wagon, were soon talking back and forth about climbing windmills and the fun of seeing farther than a person can with feet on the ground.

"You can help me," Jonas was saying, "by climbing up and bringing me the oil or whatever as I need it."

Andy licked his lips, smiled, and leaned forward with a hand on his knee.

Back inside the old Riordan house, Jocelyn built a fire in the kitchen stove after cleaning out the ashes. Outside, she took the bench from the back porch and set it in the yard, placing a tub there for rinse water. She placed a second tub on the stove in the kitchen and filled it with water bucketful by bucketful to heat. Ida Kurella had taken her broom from the wagon and was sweeping the main room like she was beating back a terrible menace.

"You don't have to do this, Ida. We just meant to ask for water. I don't mean to keep you here, take you from your own work at home."

"If you plan to catch the afternoon train tomorrow for home, it's going to take us both to get the cleaning done. I don't mind. I like to do for other folks and make friends. Open the front door there, and I'll sweep this out and off the porch for now. There must be a dustpan somewhere. You take the broom and sweep the next room while I look. I'll mop this one. Soon as the wash water is hot, one of us can wash the bedding. The other one can slosh them in the rinse water. We can wring the sheets and blankets out together and hang them on the line."

"If you say so. I admit I appreciate the help. Your son's help, too, out there on the windmill." He stood on the windmill platform working at something with a wrench. She'd watched as he climbed to the platform and laid out his tools on the bag they'd been carried in. Andy had climbed up the tower after him to the platform and handed each tool to Jonas as he asked and reached for them. Andy had been climbing windmills at home for some time now and it had bothered her a great deal for a while. Pete cautioned her not to make a fraidy cat of their son. He needed to know windmills if he was going to be a rancher. "He might even want to be a professional windmiller when he's grown." The windmill here on the Riordan property was not as high as those at Nickel Hill Ranch, and she was thankful for that.

Ida came to stand beside her. "He's a caution, how good Jonas is working on windmills, and he's always careful."

From Jonas's mother's expression, Jocelyn knew she'd read her mind. "I'm glad of that, that he's careful." She took the broom.

"Has to be. Now don't you worry, Jocelyn."

"Oh, I won't." But she did take a peek at the windmill every so often as water heated on the kitchen stove for the cleaning they had to do, and in the meantime, took to sweeping floors. In time, the oiling and repair was completed, and both boys were on the ground. The windmill's wood rotary blades creaked in the brisk wind. The sucker rod added a melodic thump and rattle lifting water from the underground to spill through a pipe into the cistern. It was the windmills' workings gentle music *creak clonk, creak clonk, creak clonk,* that Jocelyn loved and appreciated.

An hour later, Jocelyn and her neighbor, Ida, were busy scrubbing bed linens on a washboard tilted in the washtub, rinsing in the other tub of clear water and hanging wash on the line. The day had heated up and with the warm wind blowing, the bedding would be dry in an hour or two, at least.

Jonas started singing "Git Along Little Dogies," and Jocelyn smiled to herself. He'd stowed his tools and pumped water at the well until it came out clean and cool. He looked up, more than a little prideful, at the churning blades of the windmill, making background music to his singing, almost keeping in tune. Andy, who'd found an old worn broom, was cleaning the back porch, industriously if not perfect. He stopped and joined Jonas singing the song in his young boy's voice, to Jocelyn's surprise. She smothered a laugh, hadn't been aware he knew the song, although she'd heard him singing others he'd picked up from Rom, mostly. From Asa and Web, too. Heaven knew the song had been around since right after the Civil War and cattle were first driven from Texas to Kansas on the Chisholm Trail. He ought to know it.

A cyclone of cleaning continued through the rest of the day, floors were swept and mopped, cobwebs cleared from ceiling corners with a broom. Furniture polished with cloth and beeswax to a shine, surprising Jocelyn how beautiful the tables, chairs, cabinets, whatnot shelves and picture frames were. Kitchen cupboards were washed inside and out, dishes and utensils washed and replaced. When the ashes cooled, Jocelyn dug them from the stove with a scoop she'd found by the porch wood box and dumped the outside several paces away from the house. She was left feeling covered with ashes and soot, cobwebs from earlier in her hair but it was a job that needed doing. The inside of the oven and burners had already been scraped and washed clean.

Washing windows came last, but they reflected the setting sun brilliantly. Before going back inside, she followed Andy who wanted to show her the dugout in a small group of spindly trees not far from the barn. The wooden door to the stone cave didn't budge, so she let it be. "Next time we come, maybe we'll have a look and clean it, too. It'd make a nice cool place for Nila and John to store potatoes, onions, canned fruits, and the like."

They headed for the house where Jocelyn fell into a chair, tired in every inch of her body but more than pleased. Ida sagged into another chair, sighing deeply, elbows on her knees and her hands cupping her dirt-smudged face. "Well, we've done the place up fine, haven't we? You and the boy come on home with me and Jonas, and I'll fix you supper."

"Goodness, Ida, you've already helped so much, we can't accept your offer to make us dinner. I still have sandwiches and an apple or two. Now the windmill and well are in operation, we'll have fresh water to drink, and I'm desperate for a bath. You and your son have done more than enough for us and I'll be forever thankful. But no way in Hannah will I agree to your cooking for us, too."

Ida smiled tiredly. "Alright, I accept your kindness

in turning my offer down. As far as the work today, it gives me pleasure to accomplish something like this"— she motioned a circle of the newly clean room—"for someone. Makes me feel good, doesn't it you?"

Surveying the room, Jocelyn laughed and clapped her palms together. "Yes, it does. I feel fine. The young couple who'll be here soon are going to appreciate what we've done, and that makes me happier than I can say."

"Alright then, son and I are getting on home. I hope we meet again, Jocelyn. I've enjoyed your company."

They hugged tiredly. Jocelyn was thinking how fortunate Nila and John were going to be with neighbors like Ida Kurella and her family. And how the world, in general, was better off due to such people— she had many among her friends. On the other hand, the Scott brothers were the bane of her life. For the time being, they were thankfully behind bars. And, remembering what they'd done to Andy, it wouldn't bother her if they died there, like he might've, tied up the way he was in the tumble of the shack. Until, with luck, he was found.

~

Time passed quickly, and the day came for Nila and John's train to arrive in Skiddy. Pete drew their team and double buggy to a stop in the shade off the road near the train station. He smiled big. "Everybody off the wagon. I'll tie the team."

Jocelyn climbed down, smoothed her best dress, blue with tiny white flowers, collar, and puffed sleeves trimmed with lace, and swallowed the shout of glee that bubbled inside her. Nila and John would be here soon.

They were going to have a baby. Could life be any better?
She slipped her arm through Pete's as they walked
nearer the station, Andy hopping and leaping ahead.

From the time Nila had come to live with them,
she'd been an important, cherished member of their
family. Always good-natured, a help when needed.
She'd never given them a problem, although Jocelyn
couldn't say that about her mother, Flaudie, who was as
bothersome as a charley-horse in both legs at one time.
So different from her mother. Now Nila was married to
a nice young man, a baby on the way, a wonderful
future ahead of them. A future here in America, thank
Hannah. Relief filled Jocelyn, that the pair of them
would no longer be in danger particularly to a far-off
foreign country. Those worries ended right now, with
the sound of the train's whistling approach to the
Skiddy Station.

Minutes later, the train ground to a chugging,
whistling stop on the tracks and sat blowing steam. The
conductor climbed down and walked back to the
baggage car to unload while passengers began to
descend from the train to the station platform. Ten or so
passengers alighted before Nila appeared on the train
steps. No sign yet of John. A stout woman, her face like
a very ripe peach, rudely pushed aside others trying to
leave the train, rushed at Nila and grabbed her arm.
Nila shook her head and said something to the woman
and tried to pull away. The woman's hand holding Nila
was like the clamp of an alligator's mouth.

Jocelyn hurried to Nila, grabbed the woman's arm
and yanked her away so hard the woman fell back on
others trying to descend the steps leaving a sudden
mash of bodies.

"What in the name of Hannah are you doing to my cousin? Heaven forbid—" She saw John then hurrying through the churn of people coming onto the platform. "John, come help Nila. I don't know what's going on, but this person"—she pointed to the woman getting awkwardly to her feet—"is grabbing and holding her, like trying to hurt her. Snatch her handbag...something."

John took the woman's arm and steadied her. "I told you on the train that we are in no condition to give you a story for the *Wichita Gazette*. It's been a very long trip and we're tired. My wife is with child. She needs to rest. I promise we'll give you a story about our trip to Europe, another time. Her family is here to take us home. Now, we have to get our baggage and go. Good day." He turned to Nila and took her in his arms. "I'm sorry, sweetheart. The fellow with her was holding me up in the train, wanting an interview. Some journalists have to be practically hit on the head to get them to leave you alone."

Jocelyn gaped, chin in hand. "You mean that woman was wanting to—talk to you about your time in Europe, for a newspaper story about you two?"

"Exactly."

"Well, I'll be. The lady was awfully rude. I suppose that I was, too." Only a little regretful, her hand went to her breastbone in worry. "Nila, are you alright?"

Nila smiled. "I'm fine, Jocelyn. Thanks for coming to my defense. The lady just wouldn't listen to me, that I wasn't up to an interview right now. To tell you the truth, I want more than anything to spend tonight at Nickel Hill and maybe wait to make the trip to our house in Cloud County tomorrow."

Jocelyn wrapped her arms around her in a hug. "I've been wanting to do this for months, Nila, honey. I couldn't be more pleased that you and John are home here in Kansas. You may spend long as you want to at Nickel Hill. We'd love it."

"John and I have already talked. It's what we want. Just a day or two." She sagged against him, and he pulled her close.

He looked worried and kissed her cheek. He looked at Jocelyn. "Yes, we'd like to join you, give my wife a good rest."

Nila looked up at him with a wan smile. "We need to get our luggage, John." She said to the others. "We've brought quite a bit, I hope it'll fit in the buggy with the five of us." She headed to a nearby bench and sat down.

Jocelyn, lips pressed together in concern, took note. She went to the bench and sat down beside Nila and took her hand in hers. "Don't worry, we have a new double buggy. You know, a bigger buggy with two seats and a canopy over it all? We're going to take care of you, sweetheart, and that little one you're carrying. Everything will be fine."

Nila leaned against her. "I know. That's why I'm so glad to be here."

Jocelyn beamed a smile at John and Pete when they came back loaded down with luggage and bags. She waved her hand in the direction of their buggy parked a short distance away. "Let's get loaded up, everybody. Supper is waiting at home."

TWELVE

"You mean the Scott brothers' trial is finally set for sure? It's going to happen now and soon? Just thinking about them gives me the cold shivers, Pete." Jocelyn looked at him, standing by the back door, ready to go out to evening chores. She continued, "Surely they won't be found innocent this time and will be permanently jailed, taken to the State Prison in Topeka." Good things were happening in their lives, like Nila's coming baby and having her and John back in America, the ranch doing well. It'd be downright intolerable to worry again that they might lose their ranch, their young son, possibly their lives.

"The trial will go through for sure, this time, from what I hear in town. The judge has appointed a lawyer to represent them. A new fella in Skiddy, just out of law school and anxious to take on any case, steamed to get his career going. The trial is set for next month, February twentieth. If they don't break out of jail or some other stupid kablooey before that, they'll find themselves in the State Prison in Topeka for the rest of their lives."

Jocelyn held herself tight. "Praise God, anything but not set free."

He came over and drew her into his arms. "It's going to be alright, honey. Don't worry yourself."

"I'll try not to. I certainly have happy things to do, getting ready for Nila's little one."

"You do that. I have a deep feeling that the Scotts brothers will surely get what they have coming, finally."

In the next weeks, Jocelyn spent every spare moment, mostly in the evening after dinner, crocheting a baby coverlet, a jacket, bonnet, mittens, and booties, cutting out and sewing nighties. News from Nila and John indicated they were happy in their little house, making a few adjustments including a telephone. They had thanked her profusely for readying the house. Which she considered a small chore, a happy day spent with what would now be Nila and John's neighbors, the Kurella family, good people.

Come February eighteenth, and the Scott trial was delayed once again, to Jocelyn's deep disappointment. The new lawyer in Skiddy, his name, Oran Adams, had contracted severe pneumonia, with no substitute available to take his place. Jocelyn had so wanted for the situation to be over completely.

At least, she reminded herself, the culprits were still behind bars. Rather than bang her head on the wall, she'd keep her mind happily on Nila's baby's arrival in April. Nila would be coming to stay a week at Nickel Hill for that occasion, possibly John, too. She'd keep busy as possible in the meantime, make time go faster.

~

The phone was rarely used at Nickel Hill, and when Jocelyn was inside and it rang, it'd often startle her, as it did just now and so blessed early in the morning. *Ring, ring, ring.* She had to admit the phone was occasionally useful, at other times a nuisance and not a toy like it was for women who liked to be on the phone day in and day out, chatting. She picked up the receiver, "Hello?"

"Jocelyn, I'm wondering if maybe you can get away and come be with me today?"

"Oh, my goodness, Nila, yes, I'll do that. There's nothing wrong, is there?"

"I'm not sure. The baby's not due 'til next month, but I've been having strange twinges. I called the doctor to ask him to see me, but he's out of his office until later this afternoon. The person I talked to asked me to describe what I was feeling. She said it was most likely false labor. That that often happens and can continue off and on for weeks."

"Where's John?"

"In Topeka, at the paper."

"I'm coming on the train. In the meantime, ask your neighbor, Ida Kurella, to come be with you. She's good as gold at something like this. She'll know if you're in labor or not and be company if needed. Love you, Nila. I'll be there as soon as I can." She hung up the phone, tore off her apron, went for the bag of baby things she had ready, grabbed her handbag, and checked that she had money for the train. Pete was down in the barnyard, cleaning machinery for spring work. She wrote him a note telling him where she'd gone and what food in the icebox he could heat up for him and the hired men.

"Andy, you need to come with me. Change into a shirt and pants not so raggedy."

He turned from his breakfast. "I don't want to go this time, Ma. Pa said we might go fishing sometime today, the water in the creek is beginning to warm up."

She was of a mind to argue but didn't feel up to it. In the past she would have taken him to stay with Mabel Goody but she didn't have enough time to take him there and he hated to be thought a 'baby' anyway, his eighth birthday coming soon. The Scott brothers were no danger to them at present.

"Alright," she said tentatively. "As soon as you're finished with breakfast, you go to where your father is and tell him that I've taken the train to Nila and John's. Their baby might be coming. And ask him what you might do to help here around the yard or in the barn. If you'd like to spend time in the house, that is alright, too. Just don't wander off the place, whatever you do. Promise me now that you won't."

"Promise." He wore a wide grin. "And I'll do some work for Pa. I'll go tell him right now that you have to leave and I'm stayin'. To work and maybe go fishin'."

Later, on the train, Jocelyn was bothered by every stop it made. Why were folks so lackadaisical getting off and on the train? Why the lengthy conversations from some folks with the conductor before entering and then dawdling when choosing a seat? The worst of all, how long it took, at one stop, for the train to take on a load of wood and water for the steam engine. She was going out of her mind as the train chugged slowly along, with too many stops. And Nila ahead, having contractions that could be false labor, or maybe the real thing. Alone.

Doing the best she could to relax, Jocelyn told herself that Ida would be there to comfort Nila and help with the delivery should the baby be coming sooner than expected. There was a possibility that the doctor was back to his office in Hollis and had hurried on to see Nila and was with her now. Jocelyn's mind rattled on. For extra help, she should have brought Mabel Goody with her. Mabel was a most competent midwife. She'd delivered Andy and dozens of other babies for mothers in the neighborhood. Why hadn't she thought of that sooner? She shifted in her seat, her feet bouncing as if it'd hurry the train faster.

At the Hollis station, she grabbed up her bag, rushed off the train, grabbed her skirt with one hand and held the bag in the other and hurried along to Nila and John's house past the far end of town. When she reached their farm, it startled her that there was no wagon or horse that Mrs. Kurella or some other neighbor, or John, might've ridden in the yard. Maybe in the barn? There was no doctor's buggy or horse. Could they have possibly come? Everything was fine. Maybe false labor, and they'd left? She raced across the yard and onto the porch. As she reached for the doorknob, Jocelyn heard a sound from inside. A baby's fierce little cry. Her heart almost stopped and tears rushed to her eyes. Her heart hammered as she opened the door and rushed to the bedroom. Shocked at the sight of Nila all by herself except for the tiny squalling baby.

Nila's face was blanched white. There was blood on her hands and bedding, smears of blood on the tiny wailing infant lying on her stomach. Nila's hand wobbled as she held a knife toward Jocelyn. "I-I was trying to cut the c-cord. W-would y-you?"

"You poor dear girl, all alone giving birth to this dear baby girl. Are you alright? How do you feel?"

"B-better now that my baby is here and alive. S-so glad y-you're here. She n-needs washing and a-a blanket —I'm so tired. But fine."

Jocelyn fought back tears as she took the knife, set it aside, and redid the clumsily tied string on the cord. She brought a bucket from the kitchen, cut the cord, and gathered the afterbirth into the pail. She retrieved a baby blanket and wrapped the infant, held her to her cheek a few minutes to soothe her crying, then placed her next to Nila.

"I'm putting the teakettle on to heat water for a washup. I'm so sorry I wasn't here for you in time, Nila. That no one was. I expected your neighbor, Ida Kurella, to be here or the doctor by now."

"I called to ask Mrs. Kurella to come." Her voice was so shaky and soft that Jocelyn had to lean close to hear. "Sh-she and her husband weren't home. Their boy said they, and his sister, were gone to Topeka for-for the weekend." With a trembling hand, Nila wiped her sweaty hair back from her face. "The doctor, his name is Dr. Blevins, will be here soon as—as he can. John, too, on the next train from Topeka." She took a moment to draw slow, deep breaths. "I believed the mild pains were fake labor like I was told. Then they were coming so hard and fast there was nothing I could do but—let my baby girl come." She smiled. "Isn't she b-beautiful with John's dark wavy hair, my blue eyes? I planned to name her April, for the month she was b-born. I still might, if John agrees."

"I think that would be perfect. And yes, she's the most beautiful little thing I've ever seen. I'll give her a warm bath, and diaper and dress her in one of the nighties I brought, put her in the bassinet I see over there. Then we'll get you bathed, into a fresh nightgown, and fresh sheets."

A little more than an hour after those tasks were completed, Dr. Blevins, a slender fellow probably in his fifties, with a thoughtful, calm voice, arrived and took over. By then, Nila was nursing the tiny baby. The doctor, his stethoscope in hand, looked at Jocelyn.

"Would you hold the infant while I check the mother? This won't take long."

Jocelyn took the baby in her arms and held her close, pacing back and forth, then leaving for the next room. She whispered against her tiny face, "Who are you to me—second cousin? That makes me laugh. Grandchild, now that sounds ideal to me. You're my baby granddaughter if your wonderful Mommy says 'yes, that'll be alright.'" At a knock on the front door, Jocelyn hurried to open it, the baby in her arms.

A stranger, a woman, stood there with huge, dish-towel-covered baskets in each hand. "I'm a neighbor. I saw you come. I didn't know it was any more than a visit until I heard the new baby crying when I was out in my yard. Then I saw Dr. Blevins arrive in his buggy. I went around the neighborhood to collect food for you all. Chicken and noodles, steak and gravy, canned apricots, green beans and ham, warm homemade bread. Iced ginger cookies. We know how busy a time like this is for people on a birthing day." She placed the baskets inside the door. "I don't want to bother, I'll go now, but can I just have a peek at the babe?"

"Of course." Jocelyn gently took the blanket away from the teensy face.

The woman clasped her hands. "My, so tiny and beautiful!"

"April is all of that."

"You're the grandmother?"

Jocelyn hesitated, gently rocking the tiny bundle now quiet in her arms. "Yes. April is my grandbaby." *Sort of.*

A short while later, the door burst open and John, a stricken expression on his face, sailed across the room to the bedroom so fast that he didn't see Jocelyn in the corner with his baby, a small bundle against her chest. She whispered with a smile to the infant, "We'll let him have a minute or two with Momma, then we'll give your daddy a surprise meeting with his special baby daughter."

She listened outside the bedroom door for a moment. John was telling Nila that he'd asked for a vacation now rather than wait until summer. He'd be here for her and the baby and begin a little farming, too. Make repairs on the barn and fencing for a cow, get the chicken house ready for a few chickens. He'd do some writing from home, a column about the funny side of politics or some such, once a week for the *Topeka Daily Tribune*. Which, if people came to like it, he would continue writing from home. A column and any other big story in this region that the paper wanted covered. Jocelyn kissed the baby. "You lucky little thing. Not only do you have a wonderful mother, you've a purely magnificent papa, too." She tapped lightly on the door and went in.

~

A few days later, out of curiosity, while the baby was sleeping and John and Nila engaged in personal chat, Jocelyn explored the stone-lined dugout that had been John's great-grandparents' first home in Kansas. It was cool inside, and musty. She was surprised to see a few pieces of old shabby furniture. A rope bed with a thin feather mattress and a patchwork quilt of faded colors. A table and two rickety chairs, a cupboard's open shelves with dusty jars of canned fruit and vegetables, a lantern and two candles on top of the cupboard. A dusty stove with two burners, the stove pipe up through the dirt ceiling and an ancient calendar on the wall. A pair of large stone jars in the corner, one holding sticks of wood kindling.

She wandered next through the barn, noting with satisfaction that it had been cleared of old hay, calcified manure, and moldy grain. Leaving the barn, chickens fluttered out of her way, the cow lifted from grazing to look at her, chomping away at the grass she'd pulled free. Jocelyn slipped quietly through the kitchen door a short while later, not wanting to make a sudden sound that would wake baby April. John was at the kitchen table drinking a cup of coffee.

"I explored the dugout and was surprised to see it still furnished," Jocelyn said quietly. She took a chair across from John and settled her skirts. "Looks as though someone might still make it their home."

John grinned. "I've considered cleaning all that stuff out, but then I remember Grandma saying more than once that she remembered how hard life was, homesteading. Everybody stuffed in one small underground room. She decided to keep it that way as long as she lived, as a reminder of how lucky she was to live in a frame house. She changed nothing about it, and it might be a while before I can move anything in there from its spot."

"If it were mine, other than a cleaning, I'd leave it just the way your grandma wanted."

"I intend to. I remember Grandma saying that there were still a half dozen uses for the dugout. Storage for garden vegetables, a safe place to run to from a crazed bull on the loose, or a prairie fire. Sit out a storm, or to spend time in it to cool off on an extra hot summer afternoon."

"Truth to tell." Jocelyn laughed. "Kansans are best off with a dugout on their land."

The next few days, Jocelyn was in her glory, caring for the baby and allowing Nila bedrest, cooking and tidying up the house. Before long, of course, she'd have to return home to Pete and Andy and her work at the ranch. In the meantime, though, she intended to enjoy every moment that she was needed here at Nila and John's.

THIRTEEN

J ocelyn entered Nila's room with a cup of tea and small plate with two sugar cookies and placed them carefully on the nightstand by Nila's bed. "There you are. A little treat to help you get your strength back."

"I don't like putting you to all this trouble, Jocelyn. For pity's sake." Nila fluffed her pillows behind her back as she sat up straighter. "I've already spent several days in bed since birthing baby April." Her hand reached out to touch the cradle on the other side of her bed where the baby girl slept. "I think it's time I was up and around and took over like I should."

"It'll be fine for you to get up and walk here in the house a trifle each day, not good yet for you to be left to care for the baby, clean house, cook meals for John, who'll be home now, working outside when he's not writing his column or out and about getting stories for the paper." She was truly concerned, and it was hard to refrain from being stern. "Think about the piles of clothes to wash and hang out, dear girl. Now with diapers added, baby blankets and garments."

"Alright, Jocelyn, I understand. But you need to be home at your ranch, too. There's a lot to do there, and I'm sure you miss being with Pete and Andy, and they miss you." Her smile was confident. "I'm feeling better every day, as I'm sure nature intended."

Jocelyn backed away, nodding and hand wadding her apron, still not convinced. It was true. She missed Andy and Pete. But as far as cleaning house, cooking meals, and helping Andy with homework for school, Mabel Goody had stepped in, taking her place at Nickel Hill Ranch for the short time she'd be gone.

Within the few days that followed, Jocelyn cleaned Nila and John's house, went to the Hollis grocery store to stock up on necessary items for the future, went to the post office to mail letters for Nila, announcing the baby's arrival to friends. She cooked dishes to preserve in the icebox for the future: butter beans and ham, chicken and home-made noodles, roast beef with potatoes and carrots, steak and gravy. The last day, Jocelyn made sure every shred of laundry was washed, dried, folded and put in place.

By that time, Nila was bathing the baby herself, nursing her while seated in the rocking chair—not in bed. She insisted on helping with preparing meals and drying the dishes as Jocelyn washed them. She was happy and insisted she was fine, and ready to be a busy wife and Momma.

"Alright then," Jocelyn conceded. "I'll be catching the train for home. But I can't tell you how much I'm going to miss you and John. And baby April in my arms.

I wish so strongly that you lived closer to us at the ranch. Or in Skiddy. Anywhere, not so far away."

Nila was silent for an overlong minute. "You know, that's something to consider."

~

A t home again on their ranch, after being away almost two weeks, Jocelyn faced catching up with myriad chores, cleaning house, hoeing weeds from the garden, making butter, mending Andy's pants and shirts, buying new items of clothing and a pair of boots for him—he was growing up so fast.

Not for anything did she regret having been the first to see and hold Nila's beautiful child, after Nila had, of course. To be with Nila as she recovered. She was only sorry she hadn't been there to help with the delivery that had to be painful and frightening for Nila, alone.

Time dragged and by the time the month of May arrived, Jocelyn missed seeing her little girl grandbaby to the point she could hardly think of anything else. She purely ached to hold her more often than months apart. She missed Nila and John, too. They needed to find a place to live closer. John had loved working at the newspaper. Surely he could find one he'd like as much and not so far away from here. She'd seen that he'd shown no eager interest in farming. Not only that, Nila needed her company once in a while, and she needed Nila's. Would it be alright to talk with them about the matter? To convince them, to their satisfaction, naturally, that they really needed to move nearer to Nickel Hill?

She was going to try. Andy would be out of school for the summer soon. She wanted to be here for him those long hot days when young boys were compelled to wander off seeking an exciting adventure, or unexpected accidents happened. If she were to take the train to Hollis she shouldn't put it off too long and she'd have to make it a short visit. At supper, she discussed her plans with Pete and Andy. Both urged her to go. They wanted Nila, John, and baby April closer, too.

Two days later, Jocelyn caught the train on a beautiful sunny morning in Skiddy. She was surprised to see, from the train windows. that the weather worsened the further they traveled toward Hollis. Feeling a trifle alarmed when they reached her destination, she stepped off the train into the midst of a strong wind that nearly tore her off her feet and a rainstorm pounding without mercy. She was soaked to the skin by the time she reached the other side of town and beyond to Nila and John's small farm. She stood dripping at their door, licked water off her lips, and knocked on the door.

"I'm so sorry." Nila pulled her inside. "I was going to meet you in our wagon and an umbrella, Jocelyn, but the weather was getting worse by the minute, and I didn't think I should take the baby out. I was hoping you'd have brought at least an umbrella with you."

"It was a beautiful sunny day at home when I left." She wiped her face and removed her rain-soaked hat and jacket. Nila took them from her, hung the jacket on a temporary line by the stove and the hat on a peg behind the door, blotting it first with a towel.

"Where's John? Out to the barn with his critters?"

"Goodness, no. He knew you were coming and you'd be with me, so he took the train to Topeka. He misses his old friends at the newspaper and I told him to go."

"I wonder how the weather is there? It's sure looking bad here. And I'm so wet I need to dry off before I hold your precious little one."

"Take a chair there by the stove." Nila spoke in a sympathetic tone. "You can help me finish a pie that I'm making for John. The pie crust is baking in the oven." She rushed on, "Have you ever made a butterscotch pie? John had a slice of one in a Topeka café and now hints for me to make him one."

"I have made butterscotch pie but not for a blue moon." She brushed back her wet hair and tilted her head, thinking. "It's a pudding filling—but you would know that. It takes a cup of brown sugar. Then mix in two tablespoons of flour, two of butter, two beaten egg yolks, and—yes, a cup of warm water." She held her hands toward the stove. "You cook that, constantly stirring, until it thickens. Once the filling is cool, you stir in vanilla and pour the pudding into your baked crust. I think it tastes wonderful covered with an egg white meringue—spread on the pudding and browned in the oven. But whipped cream is good on butterscotch pie, too."

"We're getting eggs from our hens, milk from the cow, too, of course, but I like a meringue pie and I'll have the whites of the eggs left over from the yolks I'm using in the filling. I might add the whites from another one or two eggs, I like a high fluffy meringue."

"Sounds delicious." She smiled and watched Nila take the nicely browned pie crust from the oven with the tail of her apron and hurriedly set it on a square pastry board for that purpose.

While the baby slept and Nila mixed and stirred her pie filling, Jocelyn took the opportunity to voice part of her mission for coming to see Nila and John. "You say John is in Topeka for a day or two, visiting his pals from his old newspaper job?"

Nila looked over her shoulder at Jocelyn, a frown creasing her forehead. "I worry about him sometimes, Jocelyn. I think he'd be happier working directly day to day at the newspaper. Living out here on the farm with a few chickens and a cow and writing the column and mailing it in isn't the best fit for him. Not many big, important stories around here to cover, either."

"Has he thought about finding another newspaper to work at, say closer to where we live? Like in Junction City, White City, or Council Grove, maybe? We miss you and John and the baby so much. We'd give about anything to have you living closer to us. And John happy in his work, too."

Nila set the pan of butterscotch filling aside to cool, pulled up a chair and sat down. She wiped her brow with the hem of her apron. "I think he'd jump at the chance, compared to our life here, so far. He's not a farmer, Jocelyn, and I don't think he ever will be. He's a journalist, a writer, through and through and he loves that."

While the silence inside the room ticked away, outside the winds were a howling monster. Jocelyn shook off her worry about the weather and contemplated. "Maybe, with a strong interest in journalism, he should have a newspaper of his own, like William Allen White, publisher and editor of the *Emporia Gazette*."

"I know about him." Nila brightened. "His editorial, *'What's the Matter with Kansas?'* has made him known nationally and worldwide in some instances. It was 1896 when he wrote it; he didn't care for the

Populist Party, called them 'gibbering idiots who were ruining Kansas.' 'If there had been a brick wall around the state eight years ago,'" she recited, "'and not a soul had been admitted or permitted to leave, Kansas would be a half million souls better off than she is today—' Then he finishes his incredible essay"—she sat up straighter—"'What's the matter with Kansas? Nothing under the shining sun...' Oh, yes, John would be so good with a paper of his own. Expressing his feelings, his beliefs. But how would we buy one, if we found a newspaper that needed a new owner, or establish a paper for a town without one?"

"How did William Allen White manage to do that? John ought to go visit him." Jocelyn sat forward. "I'm sure Mr. White could give him helpful information. Possibly give him a position on the *Gazette*. Emporia is a wonderful town, Nila. As you know, we were there this past summer to watch Rom in a 101 Ranch Real West Show at the fairgrounds." She added, to make her suggestion more tempting, "Soden's Grove has a wonderful park, and we had a picnic there, toured the flour mill next to the Cottonwood River. I wish you could've been with us."

"Emporia would be closer for you to travel to see us, than Hollis is, but still some distance. I don't know—maybe John and I should look into it."

They'd had the door open a trifle for fresh air and the room had darkened while they talked. It wasn't anywhere near sundown. Curious to where the sunshine might've gone, Jocelyn stood and went to the door to look out. It had gone strangely quiet outside. Too still, giving her the shivers. She turned to Nila. "The sky doesn't look right out there. I swear in the name of Hannah, a tornado is building to the west." Her throat dried. "Come here. Look at that greenish sky, the weird-looking clouds." She pointed, her hand beginning to tremble.

"It does look like a tornado. You're right." Nila's lips pressed together in a slight grimace, her eyes showing deep concern. "Do we wait and see, stay here where we are, and lie flat on our stomach under something with baby April? What? I don't trust these storms. They sometimes fade away, other times, they destroy every single thing in their path."

Jocelyn had already made up her mind, and her heart pounded. "We're going out to Grandma's dugout, is what we're going to do right now. Get the baby, Nila, and take her there, I'll be right behind you, bringing what we'll need for her, diapers, extra blanket, water. Go!"

The storm now was heading fast their way and looking worse by the second. Her heart threatened to stop as she took in the smoky funnel churning fast and raising a cloud of what had to be flying debris. She hurled back into the room to get the necessaries and to safety in the dugout.

FOURTEEN

With arms loaded, Jocelyn left the house and plunged into the windy nightmare outside, close to losing a fighting battle toward the dugout. A watery-eyed glance ahead in the direction of town shocked her to the core. Buildings were being torn apart and large pieces ripped through the air. She ducked almost to the ground, a large chunk of tin roof barely missing her. It seemed a century passed as she lay flat on the ground pushing her bundles ahead, worming her way on her elbows and knees to the dugout door, while every imaginable object churned above and around her. She reached the door and pounded hard then lay panting, desperate to be inside. Nila opened the thick door, struggling to keep it from blowing shut or off its hinges. Jocelyn crawled inside giving her bundles a hard shove. Staggering to her feet, she helped Nila close the door.

The baby lay mewing in the middle of the bed at the back of the cave, playing with her toes, far too young to know there was danger anywhere near. Jocelyn took a few deep breaths and smiled shakily in the dim light. She put her hands on Nila's shoulders, speaking as clear as she could against the roaring, crashing wind outside their shelter. "I see you found the lantern and matches. And there was oil in it, from that long ago?" She panted. "Goodness, how'd you do that, in the dark, and with the baby?"

Nila sat on the edge of the bed and motioned Jocelyn to do the same. "John and I did a bit of cleaning and fixing in here. Spider webs and all. I knew where we'd moved the bed and I could find my way around by remembering and feeling my way after I put the baby down. John saw that the lantern had oil and washed the globe. I swept and washed dishes and eating utensils, cleaned the table and chairs, washed and dried the bedding. We were going to stock it with food other than what's on the shelves over there, and water, this evening when he gets home." She brushed her hair back from her face and her teary eyes with the back of her hand. "I just hope he gets here alright, no trouble from this tornado where he is."

"Heaven only knows what he'll find when he gets here to Hollis." Jocelyn thought a moment. "I brought us a small jug of water, baby April's things, an extra blanket. I snatched a tin of Arbuckle's coffee, chunk of ham, and a loaf of bread, in case we're imprisoned in here for a long while."

"God help us if we are. Just listen! So many things are crashing against the door, I wonder if we'll even be able to move the door and get out when the storm ends."

"Somebody would look for us here, surely."

"At least it's cooler in here, and we have ventilation. We discovered a pipe up through the roof."

After several minutes of silence, Nila asked, "Do you think you could've lived in here, Jocelyn, for very long?"

She thought about it, taking a chair. "A year or two, or more, if I had no other choice. We need to remember that Kansas is a state without a lot of trees. But there were always draws in the land, and a lot of rock. Home-steaders were wise to build these dugouts the way they did. And I've seen pictures of some that show they were beautifully furnished. More than one dugout had an organ to play, even."

"Do you think we should sing, Jocelyn, or tell stories to fill this time?" She finished with a nervous laugh, a shaky smile.

"Do you feel like singing?"

"Not really."

"Well then, let's not. I'll tell a story...if I can think of one."

At a sudden, terrible crashing outside, they looked at one another, stricken. Jocelyn's heart raced, her glance jerked here and there about the room, making sure the cave wasn't involved. Nila was pale as white marble. Her voice trembled. "I-I think the tornado just took our house, Jocelyn. Everything w-we own is in th-there."

Jocelyn nodded in agreement, her hand over her mouth.

Nila's lips continued to move but Jocelyn couldn't hear what she was saying over the noise from outside. Baby April began to cry and Nila picked her up, pressing her close to her breast.

Jocelyn's ears popped. She found a chair, cleared her throat, and swallowed. Managed to get the words out. "But we're here, with the baby. We're fine. John will be alright, I'm sure, in Topeka. Pete and Andy and our hired hands will be fine at the ranch. Let's not worry until we know what's what, for sure."

They looked wide-eyed at one another, both coming to a sudden conclusion. Jocelyn spoke first. "It's dead quiet out there. The tornado must have moved on, has hopefully died out?"

"I believe it has. But I'm not moving until we can be positive the storm's over. Good and over!"

Jocelyn nodded agreement again and sat waiting, minutes ticking by, her throat dry as burnt bread.

After another fifteen minutes or so, Nila, bouncing the baby gently in her arms, said, "I wonder if we'll be able to open the door, crawl out of here."

"I dread what we'll see when we get out. I surely do."

They reached to grasp one another's hand, waiting. Breathing sharply. *Scared.*

Baby April whimpered and sucked her thumb. Nila cooed and kissed her. "Baby's hungry, I'll nurse her, then we'll leave here and hopefully find the house still standing. Or some of it at least."

"And not alone around here."

It was about an hour later that a pounding sounded on the dugout door. Followed by a muffled, "Anybody in there?"

Jocelyn went to the door and tugged it open with pushing help from the man outside. "We're here, my cousin and her baby. We're alright." She looked back at

Nila and saw that the baby was now asleep in her arms. "How are things in Hollis?" Her heart pounded.

"Not good, not good at all. I'm one of the sheriff's deputies hired to check on things. Alright if I step inside?" When she nodded, he stepped in and removed his hat. "Your house out there?"

"Mine." Nila hugged her baby. "We heard it being hit. Is it flattened?"

"Sorry to tell you that the roof is gone and one side of the house ripped off." He rubbed his arms and rocked back and forth, pain in his eyes. "Hollis was hit the hardest. The town is gone, flattened to rubble." The silence was deafening as Jocelyn and Nila, sitting stiff as stone, waited to hear more. He continued, "The Union Pacific Depot, store buildings and houses, the Midland elevator and churches were all completely destroyed." He hesitated and rubbed the back of his neck. "There was a Union Pacific train standing on a siding at the train station that was turned completely over by the wind. Nine freight cars and a passenger coach upset. All of the passengers were injured in one way or another."

Horrified, Jocelyn got to her feet, trying to halt her shaking. "I'm fine. I can go help with those hurt. You and the baby, stay, Nila." She started for the door.

"You'd best stay here, too." Their visitor moved into her path. "A rider has gone to Concordia for a doctor, only ten miles away. The sheriff came to make sure the injured weren't robbed of whatever might be left in the ruins of their place. We're busy checking on folks. Most residents survived the tornado and they're taking care of the ones that're injured until the doc gets here."

"I can help," Jocelyn protested.

He looked at her and spoke gently. "No, ma'am. The young lady here has a baby. Help her keep watch on the ruins of her wrecked house outside there, maybe bring some of what you need that's not damaged in here. Folks not hit by the tornado are pouring in from farms and ranches in all directions to help. I have to go now, but you really need to be here." He put his hat back on and headed for the door, then turned. "I suppose you both have menfolk? That'll be coming soon as they hear of this and can get here?" He added, "Both Hollis telephone and telegraph wires are down but will be repaired in a hurry. You'd be surprised how fast news travels, anyway. By fast horseback in a lot of cases."

"Alright, I'll stay." Jocelyn felt tension easing away. "Thank you, sir, so much for checking on us and letting us know where we stand."

A while later, Jocelyn stood alone outside viewing the wreckage of Nila and John's house. The roof was ripped off, the kitchen a pile of rubble, a wall lay in an up-and-down tangle of broken boards over what looked like okay furniture where two rooms used to be. Her hand covered her mouth, and she stepped back with a slow, disbelieving shake of her head. She turned then to look at what used to be the town of Hollis. She'd seen destruction from tornadoes before but nothing like this. Tears rolled quietly down her face and she wiped them away. Their visitor was right, horse and mule-drawn wagons and buggies were hither and yon among the wreckage and dust that had been the town of Hollis. People on foot searching, picking up rubble here and there and looking—for possessions, for missing people— probably both. Her heart sickened.

It was her turn. She picked her way through the

roofless remains of what had been Nila and John's home, climbing through debris to the rooms that were intact. The kitchen had been totally wiped away. A wall was gone otherwise their bedroom appeared to be hardly touched, the baby's crib, their bed, other furniture was where it should be. A wardrobe holding their clothing was still all of a piece. The sitting room remained, the beautiful old furniture showing no seeable damage other than dirt and debris from the storm.

Jocelyn returned to the dugout and gave Nila her report. "I'll stay here with the baby if you'd like to go through things, decide on the most important to you, and bring them in here. Not a great lot of space, but we can make room by moving chairs and such out of the way."

"I'd like to do that, I could use some time from this cave, but I'm also afraid of what I'll see." She handed the baby to Jocelyn. "There are papers there in the house, what's left of it, that I have to bring over. John's grandmother's will that gave him this farm. Small treasures we picked up in Europe. Dessert plates, a cream pitcher and sugar bowl we bought in Bavaria; a tattered, well-read first edition of Charles Dickens's book, A Tale of Two Cities, a few other things that I hope haven't been destroyed. For sure, I need to bring clothes over here for the time being, ours and the baby's. I'll know what else to retrieve when I see it." She wiped a hand across her forehead, wore a look of pained disbelief.

Jocelyn gave her a smile of encouragement, a flick of her hand toward the door and cuddled the baby reaching for her face. There were benefits to all this trouble, and she adored this one, the tiny baby mewing in her arms.

Nila, looking shaky and about to vomit with the collywobbles, stepped out of the dugout. She looked back at Jocelyn. "This doesn't feel real."

"We'll be alright. We really will, Nila." Under the baby's bottom, her fingers were crossed.

FIFTEEN

It was after dark when Jocelyn and Nila had completed their salvaging task, things of importance they could move over to the dugout in stacked trunks, baskets and bundles, filling most every vacant space. Crowded to the table by all they'd moved from the wreck of the house, they ate a supper of ham, bread, an ancient can of Van Camps Pork and Beans from the dugout's shelf, and coffee. "Did you know—" Jocelyn broke the silence to take their minds from the disaster. "—a man named Gilbert Van Camp created these canned beans in tomato sauce to sell to the Army during the Civil War?"

Nila gave her a wry smile. "Yes, I know. I've heard you mention that to several people."

"Fine, I'll try to remember that." She yawned and patted her mouth. "Tried to lighten the moment, is all."

When their dishes were cleared and washed, stressed from the day's experiences and tired, they turned the wick of their lantern low and placed it in the center of the table. In the faint light, soon after, they crawled under the blankets on the bed, the baby between them. All three eventually falling asleep.

Jocelyn woke some hours later and lay awake thinking about Pete and Andy. Did Pete know about the tornado yet? He'd be so terribly worried if he did know. The train was out of the question if he wanted to come to them faster than a team could get here. There was only one thing to do, stay here and wait.

The sun was barely up, and the poor cow milked from the little she could offer when a sound outside made Jocelyn open the barn door and look. It was Ida Kurella, over by the remains of the house, sitting high in the wagon beside her son, Jonas, driving the team. Mrs. Kurella's face broke into a big smile when she spotted Jocelyn coming from the barn. "You're here, honey, and alive and well. Glory be, that makes me happy, sad as I am by the tornado's destruction of the young couple's house. How are they, are they here with that little baby?" She climbed down from the wagon.

Jocelyn went to meet her, catching her hand in greeting. "We're alright, Ida. Nila's here with the baby, both are just fine. Her husband John went to Topeka and would've returned yesterday by train if it hadn't been for the tornado tearing things up at the train station. He'll likely be here sometime today, using some other way to travel from Topeka. I expect my husband, Pete, today or tomorrow. It all depends how soon they hear about the tornado's flattening the town of Hollis."

"Well, you two bring the baby and come stay with us 'til then. It'd be a lot more comfortable than the dugout and your wretched view of the smashed town." She wore a deep frown. "Fact is, you never know when another tornado will follow yesterday's storm. Kansas weather can be so unpredictable."

Jocelyn gave the offer some thought, and despite how inviting the offer was, she turned it down. "We'll stay here where our men can find us, but thank you, Mrs. Kurella. The dugout is actually not bad. John's grandmother and her family built it and it was their home until they could build the house. You know men, though, the barn was built first, I'm told."

Mrs. Kurella's chin lowered, and she made a noise in her throat. She looked up. "I was afraid your answer would be no. Can I come in and visit for a while? I brought some cookies and fruit just in case you'd want to stay here. I'd love to see the baby."

"Of course, you can come in. Come along." Jocelyn smiled and motioned. "A good visit will fill the time until our men get here."

"They're going to be shocked when they see the awful mess that poor town is now." Mrs. Kurella looked over her shoulder and motioned. "As you can see, my boy, Jonas, is over there looking it over, talking with them men."

She went to their wagon and retrieved a basket holding fruit and cookies, then waved a newspaper at her son that she was going with Jocelyn into the dugout.

Jocelyn warmed the pot of coffee and the three women sat at the table, Ida begging to hold baby April. As she took her into her arms, the baby puckered, ready to cry, then took interest in the brooch at the neckline of the woman's shirtwaist, the frown wiped away. Mrs. Kurella laughed, hugged the baby, and played with the soft curl on the baby's head. "What a dear little baby doll. I'm so glad nothing bad happened to you all in the tornado—well, I mean, injured anyone personally. Sorry the tornado about destroyed your house and everything."

"We were lucky to have the dugout to turn to." Nila took the baby and nodded for Ida to drink her coffee. "I hadn't thought much of this cave before, I can't say how much it's appreciated now. It saved us from injury, possibly our lives. It's comfortable, and roomy enough when you get used to it."

"Truth to tell, an underground cave is more protection than anything above ground." Ida sipped the cup of coffee Jocelyn had placed in front of her at the table. She picked up the basket of apples and cookies and passed them around, then lifted the newspaper. "I brought you a copy of the Concordia Blade newspaper to read, maybe later. There's quite a story in it this morning, about yesterday's tornado destroying Hollis."

Nila lay the sleepy baby on the bed, covered her lightly and came back to drink her coffee. "We'd have cream for our coffee if the tornado hadn't blown my kitchen with the ice box in it to smithereens." She frowned in exasperation.

"You have a cow then. Was it safe from the tornado?"

"We think the poor creature got blown around some. I tried milking her a while ago with little luck," Jocelyn answered with a slow, disbelieving shake of her head. "The cow was missing for a while, then showed up out of nowhere looking beat up but basically alright. The chickens the same." She grinned sheepishly. "Their feathers ruffled though."

The other women laughed. Then Mrs. Kurella asked Nila, "Your husband planning on putting in some crops, corn, wheat, hay? And you'll be rebuilding the house, won't you?"

A long silence followed. Then Nila spoke, "We didn't expect a tornado or anything like this right off, so it hasn't come up in our plans." Her smile wavered. "I'm not sure about rebuilding, but I tend to doubt that we will. My husband loved this place when he was a little boy, visiting his grandparents. He has wonderful memories." Her brow pulled in. "The thing is, he isn't taking well to being a farmer himself, although at first, he thought that he would." She finished quietly, "His heart is in the newspaper business and that's all there is to it. He's a born journalist."

"Will you sell this property then?" A sudden look of interest shone in Mrs. Kurella's eyes.

Nila lifted her palms. "I really don't know. It'd be up to my husband. As I said earlier, he does love this place. Just not the practice of farming."

"What do you think you'll do? You don't want to live in this dugout, I'm thinking."

Nila pushed her hair back from her face. "No to the dugout, as far as I'm concerned. I think John will feel the same."

Mrs. Kurella leaned toward Nila, a kindness in her expression. "If you do have to sell—and I'm sorry if you do, I'd love to have you continue as my neighbor— would you allow my husband and I first chance to buy this property? I know he'd like to have it. It's pained him all these years to see no farming here, no one living in the house."

Jocelyn looked at Nila, her heart thumping happily, and waited for her answer. *If you and John sold out, you could live closer to us.*

Nila had her tongue in her cheek, thinking. She looked at Jocelyn and pressed her fingers to her smiling lips. "I think there's a fair chance he might sell, and I'll make sure John discusses this with your husband first, Mrs. Kurella—Ida, if that's how it turns out."

For the next few minutes after their friend left, Nila sat in the rocking chair with the baby while Jocelyn read tidbits aloud from the Concordia Blade newspaper she'd left for them, chiefly about Hollis's destruction. "My goodness, listen to this, Nila. 'Mr. Gould had left the Midland elevator on the Union Pacific track when he saw it was going to rain and went back to unlock the office door, but fortunately, the key did not work in the lock and he went under the depot platform for shelter. He was just there when the elevator was crushed like an eggshell'."

"Wow, lucky man, Mr. Gould."

"I should say so. This says that a traveling salesman on the train that turned over 'was the worst injured, his head badly crushed. It is said he may die. The poor man, his poor family if he does. Here it says that the wind not only wrecked the Midland elevator but most business properties in town. And it gives a list of businesses and residences. Oh, dear—" She hesitated. "It says, 'When the Dalton home was wrecked, Mrs. Dalton, an aged lady who was sick in bed, was carried into the yard and when found was lying in the rain, unconscious. It is reported that she died last evening, but this was an error and she is still alive. Mr. Dalton was also painfully hurt." She looked at Nila's sad face. "One more story—no, maybe two."

"Go ahead, Jocelyn, I don't mind. I want to know what happened. It's all just sad."

"Truly, it is. It says that 'many persons were caught in their houses or struck by flying debris, two being killed and many injured.'" She read on. "'As soon as Sheriff Dunnock arrived, he appointed two deputies to assist him in guarding the town and goods exposed by the wreck.' We met one of those deputies. Here's a story about a fifteen-year-old boy, Fred Jeardoe, killed when the wind blew his wagon load of corn over on him." She grasped her chin and closed her eyes. She moistened her lips before continuing. "Finally, it says that the storm covered about six miles, its path being narrow, but it 'took everything before it in Hollis.' The poor town and its people."

"We couldn't have been luckier, here on our acres at the edge of town, despite the loss of our home." Nila nuzzled her baby.

"Indeed, and we'll probably be reminding ourselves of that the rest of our lives. And should."

"What's that odd, droning noise? I hope it isn't another tornado." Nila stood up.

Jocelyn, opening the door, clapped a hand over her mouth. "The noise is your husband, it's John, and he's driven up in a motorcar." In that same moment, the engine rattle and purr shut off.

"No, he couldn't be. We don't have a motorcar." Nila rushed over to Jocelyn's side and looked out.

I think you two may have one now. "Go meet him, Nila, you and the baby. He looks wildly worried."

Nila ran and John met her halfway, pulling her and the baby close in his arms.

Jocelyn gave them two or three minutes of chatter, kissing, hard hugs, and watery eyes, then went out to give John a hug herself and examine the beautiful, royal-blue Buick touring car.

"Where did you come by this beautiful motorcar, Johnny?" Nila touched the acetylene-operated headlight, the air-controlled horn, like they might break.

"It's a long story, sweetheart. Do you have any coffee? Let's go inside." He gave the wrecked house a dark look, then joined the women heading for the dugout.

They all sat quietly while John took a few sips of coffee. Nila broke the silence. "However, did you come by the vehicle, John? Did someone loan it to you? Or is it possible to hire or rent one—?"

He'd removed his hat and ran a hand through his hair. "I did ask my good friend from the *Topeka Daily Tribune* if I could borrow the motorcar. It gets forty-five miles an hour, a lot faster than a horse and rig to get here, and I was desperate to find out how you all were, so worried you might've been injured or given time, worse than that. Vince was reluctant to loan it. We hashed it out, and he said I could take the motorcar if I'd buy it. It's two years old. He'd been thinking how much he wanted the 1908 version of the Buick."

"You bought it?" Nila held the baby close, her throat clearing.

"Like I said, honey, I was desperate to get here. Yes, I bought the Buick. It's ours now." His manner was calm and satisfied. "The paper is still making money on reprints of our stories we sent from Europe, added to what I have, half enough, anyhow, to buy the Buick. It's a smooth, wonderful ride, and it'll get us where we want to go, quicker, and more comfortable in those plush leather seats. You're going to love it, Nila."

"But I do, already." She giggled.

Jocelyn laughed at them. "Life certainly makes up at times for Mother Nature's cruel tricks. Lost a house, gained a grand motorcar because of it. There was a time when I had the Skiddy livery stable, that I didn't care for motorcars, thought they were nothing but a noisy nuisance. Which at the time, they were. Right now, I envy the vehicle more than you can imagine."

"Soon as I rest a bit, I'll take you and Nila and the baby for a ride to Concordia for whatever we need to cover the next few days. When we get back, Nila can pick out a few things, maybe a piece of furniture she'd like to keep, and if Pete's willing, send it home with you in the wagon. While we're here in the Hollis neighborhood, anything left, like the cow, chickens, hay, I'll sell or give away to folks needing them."

"Thank you. I'm counting on a ride in that beautiful machine, but for the time being, I need to stay here. Pete could arrive at any time. That is if nothing drastic has happened to him."

Sixteen

Nila and John and the baby had been gone an hour and a half, or more, when Pete drove in, drawing the team up and halting the wagon at the door of the dugout. Jocelyn, in the barn trying to get milk from the poor nervous cow, saw their arrival through the open door. She stood, gave the cow a few pats, and hurried to meet Pete and Andy. *Sweet Hannah, but she'd missed them these last few days. During the uncertainty that she'd survive the tornado, especially.* Andy hopped off the wagon, ran and threw his arms about her waist. "You're alive, Momma!" He studied her face, looked at her arms and ankles. "Not hurt, either. Please come home, now. We need you at home. Pa worried about you, and I did, too."

"That's my aim, son. I want to be there with the two of you as soon as possible." She held him tight and blinked back thankful tears. "Was everything alright at home?"

"Yes, no tornadoes, just you not there when we

found out about the tornado here, and that it mashed the town to nothin'.'"

Pete, with a sparkle in his eyes and a warm grin, pulled her into his arms. "Wife, if you try to take off from home anytime in the next sixty days, I'm going to tie you to a corral post and keep you where I can see you and take good care of you."

She kissed him fiercely for a full minute. "You won't have to, I want to be home with you, Pete, and our son, more than anything. If Nila and John were here right now, I'd be saying goodbye and climbing on our wagon over there."

"They're not here?"

"They went to Concordia to buy supplies; they're going to stay here the next few days in the dugout. Clean up things, sell or give away what they don't want to keep. Which reminds me, they've put aside a few small pieces of furniture that they want, and they hope you'll be able to take them home in the wagon to store their things in the barn or somewhere at the ranch. Wait until you see what John is driving."

"Not a wagon of his own, I'm figuring."

"Right. He was desperate to come home in a hurry to Nila and his baby and he bought an autocar, a Buick, to get here."

"Nah, really? He beat me to it?"

"I'm ready for a motorcar, too, Pete. As soon as we can afford it. His auto is beautiful, shiny blue, faster than horses—John drives it twenty-five to thirty-two miles an hour, but he says it can go as fast as sixty miles an hour. Can you imagine?" She rushed on, "It's so comfortable, padded leather seats, two separate seats in front and a seat in back wide enough for three people. It has a bulb horn to let people know you're there, a top that two people can put up if it's raining, a windshield, and a speedometer. The headlights are fueled by gasoline, and there is also a side lamp fueled by kerosene. It's removable so that when you reach the barn at home, you can remove the lamp and be able to see your way to the house." She smiled, pushed her hair back and asked, "Isn't that something, Pete?"

He laughed. "Sounds pretty great, hon. We'll be looking into one'a those for us before long. Right now, I want to rest these horses an hour or two, feed and water them, rest myself. See that Buick and have a short visit with our Nila—John and the baby, then turn around with you beside me and head in the direction of home. I thought we'd try to get as far as Junction City yet today. Get us a hotel room and breakfast there, then on home tomorrow. What do you think?"

"It sounds perfect. I can hardly wait to be home again."

~

Three weeks later, Jocelyn was at home hoeing weeds from the garden, her mind in deep thought. They'd had an enjoyable visit here on the ranch with Nila and John and baby April for a week after the tornado. It was no surprise when nearly every day, friends of Jocelyn and Pete dropped by for a visit, especially to admire the Riordans' extraordinary motorcar, the beautiful blue Buick. And discuss how it ran, its price, its special advantages.

The day came for Nila, John, and baby April, to return to Topeka, the hotel where the couple had lived before traveling to Europe. Jocelyn, hating to see them go, reminded herself repeatedly that they had their own life to live. John would be seeking a new job, and the two of them determining where they'd live permanently. Which could be almost any place on the face of the earth. With all her heart, she hoped it would not be far from Nickel Hill Ranch.

At the sound of horses and rattling wagon wheels over by the house, Jocelyn looked up, and leaning on her hoe, watched a woman in a dark-green suit and large feathered hat climb down from the wagon and walk confidently her way. The stranger was tall, angular, possibly in her late forties. She looked like someone Jocelyn might've met but she wasn't able to place her.

"Good afternoon." Jocelyn looked at her inquisitively, meeting her halfway. "Have we met before? You look a bit familiar, but I can't recall where we might have got acquainted."

"We haven't met before." Gray eyes in the woman's somewhat weathered face met Jocelyn's in what looked like an apology. "I have a faint family resemblance to my brothers and—you more than know them. I've come to talk with you to ask a favor. My name is Rowena, Miss Rowena Ann Scott." She looked away for a second, then back and taking a deep breath. "I hope you'll hear me out."

Jocelyn hesitated, thinking of the grief and pain the Scott brothers had caused them. A loss of cattle, a loss of time, and worst of all—nearly the loss of their son's life. "Whatever you have to talk about, I doubt that I can help you. Do you a favor. As you must know, your brothers have gone to great lengths to make our lives miserable while trying to steal our property—

insisting that it belongs to them. When it purely doesn't."

"I know, and I want to apologize for what they've done to you.' She dragged her palms down the sides of her skirt and bit her bottom lip. "I'm not first to admit they are fools. Idiots from a young age, and I don't know why, our parents, Matilda and Emmett Scott, were good people, nothing like my brothers' their sons, turned out to be." Her face held a look of desperation, her eyes guarded and wistful. "Can we talk about this, please?"

Jocelyn's shoulders dropped. The woman was being straightforward, honest and friendly. Why not find out what it was she wanted? "I suppose we can talk." *Nothing but that should be any harm.* "Come to the porch where we can sit in the shade and have a glass of ice water."

When they'd settled in porch chairs, and Jocelyn had brought out glasses and a pitcher of water, Rowena Scott continued. "I want you to know that when I talked with your neighbor Mrs. Goody on the telephone about our old ranch, I was delighted to learn how wonderfully it was being used and growing in your and your husband's hands. I should've known better, but I had no idea my brothers would use the good news I told them against you. About Nickel Hill Ranch, the place our folks homesteaded and named. That they'd claim you and your husband had no right to Nickel Hill, and it actually belonged to them." Her jaw clenched. "The idiots, I'm really, truly sorry."

"I accept your apology. You said something earlier about a favor?" She tried to shake off a feeling of dread, crossed her arms over her stomach in a protective huddle. "What is it that you want?" Uneasy, she sat back and reached to have a sip of ice water.

"I've visited my brothers in the Skiddy jail. They hate it there, are scared out of their minds they'll end up in the state penitentiary for the rest of their lives." She held up her hand to stop anything Jocelyn might say. "I found why they wanted Nickel Hill, and it wasn't to keep for themselves. They aren't ranchers, farmers even. They wanted the ranch so they could *sell* it for whatever they could get and use the money to go to California. And make a life there owning a saloon, or some such. Run for sheriff, even."

Jocelyn's lips pursed, and she shook her head, surprised and in doubt. "That's all well and good for them, but stealing our property is hardly the way to go about it." *And won't ever happen.* She was close to telling this woman she'd heard enough, to please leave. But it was clear Rowena Scott had more to say. Jocelyn rubbed her brow and fanned herself. "Go on," she said tightly.

"I admit, you're right. Like I said, they are idiots without brains to think straight. Now then, this is my proposition. I want to make a deal with you, and with the Skiddy marshal to free them to leave Kansas." At Jocelyn's gasp, her widened eyes, Rowena held up her hand again to let her finish her piece. "I would provide the money for train tickets to California and money to start up a business." She wore a grim smile. "I know you're thinking that's not a fair thing to do and how could I afford it, anyway. Well, this is how. When Whitman Hanley Senior bought the ranch after our mother died, and the money was divided between my brothers and me, I kept mine, let it grow, and invested. I own a bakery and a café. Both are doing well. Money is not a problem." She frowned. "I don't want my brothers to know that, however. I'm going to tell them I borrowed the money from the bank."

"Wait just a minute." Jocelyn stood, took a few paces on the porch, and circled back. "I'm not sure I want to help you. Your brothers are cruel and have a senseless, slanted look on things all around. Thinking they could get your parents' ranch back through bullying, even though we could prove it was legally ours from the start. They kidnapped our young son and let him suffer alone, wounds from a tangle in barbed wire. No food or water. Hungry and tied up in a broken-down shack, where he might've died if he hadn't been found. Using him as ransom, their plan to force us to give them the ranch to get him back. One of our hired men found our son Andy in time, thank heaven." She waved a hand. "Your brothers stole our cattle, pulled every kind of wicked stunt possible to drive us out. Engaged in a vicious brawl with our hired men, trying to steal the ranch, take it over while we weren't home. Luckily, our men got the better of that insanity."

"I can't—can't argue against any of this." Rowena's voice cracked, and her eyes watered. She swiped at tears with her knuckles. "My brothers deserve punishment for all the harm they did." Her chin lifted, her expression determined. "I'm thinking that living in a cage these past months may be punishment enough, God willing. So far, for all their cruelty, the heartless trouble they've caused, they didn't kill anyone. I honestly believe that if they were free again, they'd never commit another stupid act that would put them back behind bars. I could be wrong, but I'd like to try.

I'm hoping you'll come with me to have a discussion with Marshal Hillis and his deputy wife about this, and hopefully that you and your husband will give your permission, and the marshal will agree."

Miss Rowena Scott, your proposal is as daft as your brothers have been to take Nickel Hill from us. However, if the Scott brothers realized they'd never have Nickel Hill and chose to spend the rest of their lives on the far side of the United States, it would be a near-unimaginable blessing for us here in Kansas. Even so, she could not agree to what Miss Scott wanted. At any moment, they could break free of Rowena Scott's plan and return to their determination to have Nickel Hill Ranch. She pinched the bridge of her nose and closed her eyes tight while her stomach roiled and she struggled to give a reply. She hesitated, pursed her lips and finally spoke. "I can't believe that what you suggest could be a good idea, I doubt very much that it would work."

"There's no way to know for sure before it's tried. In my soul, I think life in California will appeal to them so much Kansas will be dismissed and long forgotten."

Jocelyn sighed. "Were you thinking of taking this to the marshal yet today?"

"I was on my way to Skiddy when I decided I must talk with you first."

"Let's find my husband and get his opinion. I believe he's at the barn repairing a hay rake." She added, "I have to warn you, I believe he'll agree with me."

Pete sat on a barrel and listened carefully, most of the time scowling, other times looking sad about the whole affair. He finally gave them his answer. "After what they've done, I'd like to see your brothers on another planet, if not the gallows, Miss Scott. I reckon California could be a good plan but there's no guarantee. I'm sorry, but I can't agree to just let them go. No trial or anything. This is the law's decision. Those Scott men have made the marshal's life miserable there at the jail. He just might agree to this plan, but I sincerely doubt it." He looked at Jocelyn. "If you want to ride into Skiddy and be present when Miss Scott discusses this with Marshal Hillis, and give him our side of this, go ahead."

Jocelyn clenched her fists, wanting to stay home and continue as if none of this had come up. Her mind rambled. *Miss Scott has been fair. I'll try to be fair, too. I'd like to be there to know for certain Marshal Hillis's decision.* She looked at Pete for reassurance. He wore a serious expression and shrugged a shoulder.

She nodded and let out a deep breath. "Come to the house with me, Miss Scott—Rowena, while I change my clothes. Pete, will you keep Andy here?" She looked down and saw Andy right beside her.

"I want to stay here with Pa, not go to no jail."

"Right answer, son." Pete gave Jocelyn an encouraging smile, a look that told he was proud of her, taking a new step into this mess. She took a deep breath, smiled back and kissed her son on the top of his head.

SEVENTEEN

Seated beside Rowena Scott in her wagon rumbling along the dusty road to Skiddy, Jocelyn's thoughts continued to churn. *How fine it would be to send the Scott brothers two thousand miles away from Kansas for good. Maybe she should accept Rowena Scott's plan? She dreaded the prospect of another trial. She and Pete were expected to be there, testify against them. So were their hired men required to be there this time, testify about the day they'd fought it out with the Scott brothers who were determined to get rid of them and take over the ranch. For goodness' sake, what was she thinking, let the Scott gang go free? What if Andy hadn't been found? The hoodlums risked his life without a care in the world about his welfare. She'd had enough of the Scott brothers' torment, trying to take their ranch from them. And she was in favor of obeying the law, sick of endless worry. This had to end, one way or the other.*

When they reached Skiddy a few minutes later, climbing down from the wagon, she felt sorry for

Rowena, having the kind of brothers that they were. As they headed for the marshal's office, Jocelyn's sideward glance at Miss Scott showed that she had her own tough worries. Her jaw set—like whatever the outcome, it was clear she was going to fight on her brothers' behalf.

Marshal Hillis looked up from behind his desk when they entered. He stood up, his face showing surprise that the two women came in together. "Back to visit your brothers, Miss Scott?" He took off his hat. "Hello, Jocelyn. What brings you here today?"

"Hello, Marshal." Rowena's chin lifted. "We're here, *I'm here,* to discuss my brothers' situation and how it might be solved. For them, and you, sir."

"I'm here"—Jocelyn cleared her throat—"to give my views about the matter, and Pete's."

He halted suddenly from his task of giving them chairs. "That so?" He ran a hand down his whiskered chin, his expression wary. "Have a chair, ladies"—he motioned—"and we'll have a talk. What's this about my prisoners, your brothers?" He gave Rowena Scott a pointed look, his cheeks sucked in and his arms across his chest.

"With certain conditions, how would you feel, to let them go, into my hands?"

He laughed, looking at her in amazement. "I can't do that, Miss Scott. A case has to follow the law. They're staying right where they are."

"I understand. My brothers have made a lot of awful trouble for the Pladsons, I admit that. Not exactly big, major crimes, though. They didn't commit murder, burn anything down, nothing like that. What I propose is to put them on a train to California with an order from you that they are never to return to Kansas. That's what they've been wanting to do, go to California. Fools that they are, they thought that they could trick the Pladsons, bully them out of their ranch, convince them it actually belongs to them. Then they'd sell the ranch for whatever they could get, to make the move out west. At one time, Nickel Hill Ranch did belong to my parents, good people, lock stock and barrel. From the beginning, it's been sold legally. Everything having to do with the property later was perfectly legal. My brothers, nor me, have any right to it at all."

"I won't mind having your brothers out of my jail, I can tell you that, Miss. They've been nothing but trouble every blasted day from when I arrested them. They yell, argue and fight with one another, complain about the food, harass Cora when she's doing the best with their meals. It's costing the town money to keep them here. The trial has been put off time and again, hardly a lawyer around is interested in representing them, defend them at a trial. Dam—darn right, I look forward to being rid of them. That'll be one of the best days in my life, Miss Scott. But it'll be done legally."

Rowena grinned as though she'd only heard what he'd said first, and counted on that. She leaned forward, her expression growing serious. "I'm in a position to buy their train tickets to California and provide money for them after they get there. It would be up to you to put them on the train, handcuffed, marched every step of the way to the station and onto the train. I'd be there to tell them it's my doing. Unless they want to return to their jail cell, they are California bound. I would bet my life they'll grab the chance to do what they'd been desperate for, all along." She waited, looking concerned but hopeful.

The marshal looked at Jocelyn. "And what do you think of this arrangement? You and Pete and your son were the victims of their wrongdoing. Took the brunt of every mean trick they pulled, the laws they broke."

Jocelyn was silent a moment. She spoke quietly, her words in earnest. "All true and the very reason we want to see them out of our life. Pete and I believe they deserve to go to prison. Allowing them to be free to go to California as they've wanted is like giving them a gift for their wrongdoing. And what if they left the train at a stop on the way, turned around, and came back? I feel sorry for Miss Scott. I can't agree to any such plan, nor will Pete."

"That's good, that's good." He turned to Rowena. "Miss, I'm sorry to tell you, your brothers' futures are all but set. My wife, and deputy, Cora, caught your brothers making a plan to break out of this jail. A plan that might've worked had Cora and me didn't know about it. The way they talked, the only way to get the ranch, which they've talked themselves into believing it rightfully belongs to them, is to do away with the Pladson family. To cause some kinda accident that would—I hate for you to hear this, Jocelyn—an accident to—to send you all to your graves."

Jocelyn chilled all over, couldn't speak. Rowena looked equally shocked, frozen, and wide-eyed.

Marshal Hillis continued. "Their trial is set for next week, five days from now. I was about to call you and let you know, Jocelyn, minutes before you came in. Judge Rawlins will be presiding. After I called him and told him the Scott gang's criminal story, he made sure to get us a trial date. Miss Scott..." He took a couple steps toward her, his brow furrowed. "I feel for you, I do. But your plan wouldn't have been accepted no matter what. A person commits a crime, and your brothers committed plenty. They pay the price. The law is the law."

Rowena looked down at her feet and her voice thickened. "I tried. That's all I could do." She wiped tears from her eyes. "Can I see them to say goodbye?"

The marshal hesitated, wiped a hand across his mouth. "I'll give you a minute or two. And I'll be standing right there with you." He patted his holstered gun.

"I'll be over at Noack's store, Rowena. You can pick me up there." Jocelyn hesitated, then put her arms around Rowena in a hug. "I'm so sorry."

Rowena nodded and brushed at tears. "I know. I'm sorry, too. For all that happened to you."

The women shared few words on the drive to Nickel Hill Ranch, each deep in their own thoughts. When they finally reached the ranch, and Rowena drove up the lane to the house, Jocelyn could smell food cooking. She laughed softly. "Oh my goodness, the men must have finished cooking the dinner I started before we drove to Skiddy. I can smell hot yeast bread, they've baked rolls. And frying potatoes. Likely, butter beans and ham, too." She jumped down from the wagon. Going to the back of the wagon, she retrieved her purchases from Noack's store.

"I'm glad to have met you, Jocelyn. We might've become good friends. In other circumstances." Rowena pulled on the lines, started to turn her team of horses around to leave. "Bye."

"Wait." Jocelyn whirled, hand up, to stop her. "Come in for supper. We've had a trying day with no food. Come eat with us." She readjusted the bundles in her arms.

Rowena stopped the team but shook her head. "I can't do that. What would your husband think, after all that my brothers did to you, to your ranch?"

"*You* weren't responsible. Come on in."

"I was responsible. Without thinking, I spilled all that information Mrs. Goody told me about you and your husband and Nickel Hill to my brothers."

"You didn't know, at the time anyway, how they would use it. Mrs. Goody would be just as much at fault for sharing the information to you, but I don't blame her. How could she know that your brothers would make the decision they did, to take the ranch away from us, using what they had just learned?"

Pete had come from the house. Rowena started again to turn her team back out to the road "Don't go, not yet." Jocelyn held up her hand. She turned to Pete. "I've invited Miss Scott to have supper with us."

His look of surprise vanished quickly. "Sure, c'mon in, Miss Scott. You two are just in time. Andy's getting the plates and utensils on the table. Me and Andy caught some catfish to go with everything else. We got plenty of darn good food inside and us fellas cooked it ourselves."

Rowena's smile wavered as she climbed from her wagon, handing her team's reins to Pete when he reached for them. She rubbed a hand on her shirtwaist and over her heart. "You folks are kind to do this, invite me."

"Our pleasure," Jocelyn said, leading the way to the house.

Andy flinched, and his face turned white when he saw who was with his mother. Scowled when she introduced Rowena. She gave him what she thought would be a comforting smile. "This is my son, Andy. The fellas over there are our cowboy crew, Web, and Skeeter—well, real names Webster Beatty and Asa Young,"

"Howdy, Miss Scott." Web nodded and gave her a quiet smile.

Skeeter rubbed a healing scar on his face that the Scott brothers had given him. He sighed. "Howdy."

"Hello, it's nice to meet you all." She hesitated. "If I'm making any of you uncomfortable, I understand. My brothers and all..." her voice trailed off. She licked her lips, her chin lifted. "I can leave." Her glance fell on Andy then turned to Jocelyn.

"You're staying. You're not your brothers, Rowena." She touched Andy's shoulder and ruffled his hair.

Pete came in the back door that same minute. "Hey, I thought you'd all be eating. Why are you standing around? Let's eat before the food gets cold. You're gonna like the fish me and Andy caught, right, son?"

"Yes!" Andy grabbed his chair and sat down.

Jocelyn sighed in relief, caught Pete's look of agreement.

For a good fifteen minutes or more, everyone ate in silence. Wanting to sidetrack Andy from his half frightened, half angry looks at Rowena, Jocelyn spoke up. "Andy, how was the fishing? Did you catch some yourself?"

He was silent a moment. "Every durned time I threw my line into the water, a worm for bait on the hook, a crawdad come an' took the bait. I had to get the crawdad off without gettin' pinched with its pincers. I finally caught two fish, but they was too little to keep."

"That reminds me," Web said. "About a time when my younger brother was in sixth grade. There was a crick close to the schoolhouse and during recess, he and some of his friends would head down there to fish with the pole they kept hid in some brush. Mostly they were after fish that they could take home in their lunch pails, a lunch pail being an empty lard can with a lid. Ma always washed his lunch pail each evening so it'd be ready the next day to take to school. One time she took out his thermos. You know what those are? They come out a few years back—"

Andy spoke up. "A thermos is a drinkin' thing. I got one. It keeps milk cold or cocoa hot, however you want it."

"Right," Web continued. "Our ma opened the thermos and there was a big crawdad inside, about to pinch her finger. She screamed like you can't believe, 'Timmeee!' that's my brother's name. Tim hadn't known about it. Evidently a friend had slipped it into his lunch pail when he wasn't looking."

Andy's eyes were aglow with humor and excitement. "That's a good trick."

"Not to my mind," Jocelyn said with a short laugh.

Skeeter spoke up. "I know a crawdad joke." He sat up straight, eager to share. "What do you call a lazy crawdad?"

Andy slumped back in his chair and growled. "I don't know."

"I don't either." Jocelyn shrugged and took a sip of her coffee. "Do you know, Rowena?"

"I have no idea."

Pete laughed. "Devil if I know."

"You're gonna have to tell us, Skeeter, 'cause I shur as the dickens don't know, either."

Andy looked at Skeeter, on the edge of his chair, anxious to hear.

Skeeter threw his chest out, a wide grin on his face. "A lazy crawdad is a 'slobster.'" When no one reacted, he looked disappointed. "You know, a lobster—a crawdad looks a lot like a lobster. When a person is lazy and messy, he's a slob. A lazy crawdad is a slobster."

Web groaned. Pete threw his hands up.

The rest admitted they couldn't have guessed.

Andy was laughing in delight. "A slobster. A slobster. Lazy crawdad."

Web, his eyes kindly and showing interest in Rowena most of the meal, asked, "Miss Scott, do you have any crawdad stories?"

"No, sorry. I wish I did. These have been funny." She clasped her hands together in front of her on the table. "I have a horse story if you want to hear it?"

When everyone nodded or answered 'yes,' she began.

"When I was a young girl, I badgered my pop for a long time to buy me a horse of my own. Instead, for the moment, he talked me into riding a big two-year-old calf. I got on and nothing happened. No matter how much I gave it my barefoot heels or begged it to 'getty-up,' go, darn animal. Well, my pop took over and twisted the calf's tail. The calf bucked like a wild bronc and sent me head over heels into a tangle of thistle. Pop nearly laughed himself sick. I didn't like it one bit, all the stickers in my arms and my backside."

Jocelyn tried not to laugh. "You poor thing. Your Pop shouldn't have done that."

"He felt bad about it...later." Her eyes sparkled. "An' you know what?" She focused on Andy, who was still giggling. "He bought me a horse. A pretty little pinto that I came to love dearly and rode for years. Yep. We were the best of pals, my horse and me."

Andy's expression of fear and dislike had totally gone. He looked at Rowena with young boy admiration, liking. "What's your pinto's name, ma'am?"

"Jolly. I named him Jolly—maybe because we had such good times together."

Andy gave her a big grin. "I have a lot of fun with my horse, Lightning, too. He's not real fast, but kinda."

After Pete finished his account of how he caught the fish they'd eaten, Rowena got to her feet. "I'll help you clear the table, Jocelyn. Then I must be going." She looked at everyone around the table. "You all have been so kind to me. It's been a long time since I've enjoyed a supper this much. Thank you, for everything." She set her chair away.

"Can't you stay, Rowena, for dessert?" Jocelyn pushed back in her chair and stood. "I bought a lemon cream pie from the bakery section of Noack's store." She hesitated. "Matter of fact, you're welcome to spend the night."

"I really can't. It'll take me time to get back to Skiddy, I'll spend the night in the hotel and be off for home before daylight. But thank you for the offer."

Pete brought Rowena's team and buggy up from the

barn. Jocelyn, Andy, the hired men, all stood by outside, seeing Rowena off.

"She's not a bad person." Web was the first to speak when she'd turned from the end of the lane onto the road to Skiddy.

"Not like her brothers, that's for sure," Skeeter added.

"I like her, I wouldn't mind having her for a friend." Jocelyn smoothed her hair back.

"I wish I coulda seen her horse, Jolly," Andy mumbled wistfully. "She's a nice lady."

"Sure seems so." Pete's brow wrinkled as he watched Rowena disappear into the distance, then he turned to follow Web, Skeeter, and Andy as they headed for the barn and evening chores.

With a huge sigh of relief, Jocelyn shook her apron high to cool her face and headed for her kitchen. She couldn't be more thankful that the Scott brothers would go to trial and then to prison, hopefully for several years.

EIGHTEEN

Would she ever catch up with her work? Jocelyn put her hoe away in the shed by the barn, hoping that it was the last bit of planting garden this year—squash, pumpkins, more potatoes. The peas she'd planted in early spring would be ready before long to pick, shell, and can. In her never-ending chores already this morning she'd fed the chickens, milked Trudy her cow, mixed a batch of yeasty bread and put it to rise on the table in a ray of sunshine through the kitchen window. Next was doing the washing, folding clothes and putting them away, scrubbing floors. Darning socks, sewing buttons on shirts, and cutting carpet rags. In the midst of all that, cooking three meals a day. And when needed, taking dinner and water to the men working in the fields.

That reminded her of a neighbor woman back where she and Grandma Letty used to live, in the Neosho River Valley, near Bushing. On a steaming hot day, right before threshing their hundreds of acres of wheat, the woman dressed to go to town. Shockingly refused her husband's orders for her to stay home and tend her job, cooking and serving a dozen men, threshers who'd need their noon dinner. No amount of begging convinced her to stay. Off she went. Jocelyn rubbed her aching back on the way to the house, feeling a giggle bubble up. *It was probable that woman had cooked and sweated through one harvest too many.* Anyhow, that's what Gram said at the time.

In her own case, Jocelyn decided getting behind was her fault. Traipsing off to Hollis to spend time with Nila, John, and the baby, because her heart missed them terribly. Getting caught in a tornado—who knew that would happen? Needing to stay until travel was clear. Then, just the other day, leaving her own work undone and joining Rowena to discuss the matter of the Scott gang with Marshal Hillis.

To be honest, she'd do any of that again in a heartbeat. Life shouldn't be all work.

An hour or so later, Jocelyn was hanging wash on the line when a horse nickered in the direction of the lane. She turned to look, and blocking the sun from her eyes with her hand, stared. As they drew closer, she recognized the young man on a beautiful black and white horse, Rom! The other rider, on a dark reddish horse, was a young woman in a tan divided skirt and white shirt. A brown wide-brimmed hat settled low, her face shadowed except for a shy smile. *Am I seeing things?* Jocelyn took the clothespin she'd been about to use from her mouth and started in their direction. "Rom, son, you always surprise me. It's blessed good to see you. And your—your friend?"

His grin grew wide. "Awful good to see you, too, Ma." He nodded at the girl on the other horse. "I brought Lara Ann to meet you. Lara Ann Yost, but her last name's about to change." He swung from the saddle, walked over and took the girl's hand after she dismounted and brought her over to Jocelyn. "Ma, she's more than a friend. Me and Lara Ann came here to get married."

Elation mixed with doubt radiated through Jocelyn's body to the point she didn't know what to say. Lara Ann hesitated and then held her hand out for Jocelyn's. "It's nice to meet you, Mrs. Pladson. Rom, here"—she looked at him with a warm, affectionate smile—"told me that you're a wonderful second Mom to him." Her smile wavered. "You don't mind that Rom and I came here to get married? Do you?" She looked a trifle worried.

Jocelyn shook her head. "No, no, not that. But aren't you both—so young? To get married?"

Rom, laughing, reached and hugged Jocelyn. He leaned back, studying her face. "Ma, I'll be twenty-one my next birthday. Lara Ann is eighteen. We've cared for each other from the time we met, both riding for the 101 Ranch. We love one another a heap and for good. There's no reason not to get married."

"Al-alright, son, but let's go in the house and talk about it."

"You two go ahead." He motioned them toward the house. "I'll put our horses up and be right with you."

"I'll help you finish hanging your wash while he does that." Lara Ann headed briskly toward the basket of wet clothes. "Looks like it'll only take us a minute or two."

For a brief second, Jocelyn stared. Was this the help she'd been needing since Nila married and began her own new life? Well, maybe not, if Lara Ann Yost and Rom were truly getting married with a home of their own. Still baffled by this sudden announcement from Rom, she joined Lara Ann hanging the rest of the wash.

In the living room a short time later, Jocelyn brought them iced tea. She sat down, sipped her tea. "Now, what's all this about getting married, Rom? It'll take a lot of planning. You've picked a date?"

"We've picked day after tomorrow for our wedding day. A few things to do first."

Jocelyn clapped a hand over her mouth, eyes wide. *What in the name of Hannah were they thinking? Day after tomorrow? When I have so much to do, and Pete and I will have to leave for Council Grove and the Scott gang's trial?*

"Here in the yard, like Nila and John did, if that's okay," Rom continued. "But we just want ours to be a small wedding, us and family. A lot of guests, like how many came to Nila and John's wedding, took too much work. Especially for you, and we don't need or want that, Ma."

Lara Ann nodded. "A small wedding will do us fine." She took her hat off, showing thick, dark curly hair tied up in a ribbon in back. She waited expectantly.

Jocelyn started to protest and Rom stopped her, repeating, "It's how we want our wedding, Ma. In the morning, Lara Ann and me are going into Skiddy to get our marriage license and find us a preacher."

Of all things, they want a wedding like Pete and I had, Jocelyn realized all of a sudden. *Francina, owner of Nickel Hill Ranch after her son died, had wanted Jocelyn to stay on and continue to manage the ranch where she'd been abandoned with a herd of mules. And if Jocelyn married Pete, the two of them could manage the ranch together. Although they argued that it wasn't necessary, Francina had already decided to leave the ranch to Jocelyn in her will.*

I reckoned, on the spot, it was perfect that Pete and I should get married that very day. And we did, with Francina Gorham and her friend, Olympia, as matron of honor and bridesmaid. Pete's best friend, Red Miller, for his best man.

"You're sure a small wedding is what you want, Lara Ann?"

"Yes, Mrs. Pladson, I do. I don't need all the fussy stuff. My grandma said, more times than I can remember, to my sisters and me, 'What's more important is the marriage, the couple's life together, and having a family to love. Not the wedding, that's just a little thing, though the promises you make to one another, now that's more special than anything else.'" She smiled confidently, her brown eyes shining.

Jocelyn took deep breaths, gratified. "Alright then, I suppose that settles it. A wedding here, day after tomorrow."

"Where is Andy?" Rom asked suddenly.

"Peter, on his way to town to help George Jacobsen at the sale barn, dropped him off at the Webbers'. I should've been the one to do that, but we decided I had too much to do here at home. Andy'd been invited earlier to spend a couple days with the Webber youngsters. They'll bring him home tomorrow evening. He'll be crazy happy to see you, Rom."

"Suits me." He grinned. "Maybe Lara Ann and I can pick him up on our way home tomorrow? Now that would surprise him."

"It sure would, if you intend to do that."

The next day, after Jocelyn had done her morning chores and was ironing before the day turned hotter—and Rom and Lara Ann got back, bringing Andy—she wanted to bake a wedding cake, at least that. A small pretty one, but nothing fancy. When she thought about it, though, she and Pete hadn't had a wedding cake and never gave it a second thought. She laughed out loud. Whatever would be, would be.

She was quite glad she'd given the house a good cleaning yesterday before they'd arrived. In case Rom and his love, Lara Ann, did invite a few folks to come. Rom had friends in and near Skiddy, and he was well acquainted with her and Pete's friends. Maybe she could get Web and Skeeter to make homemade ice cream again, like they did for Nila and John's wedding.

Thinking about the latter, she went to the phone and called Nila. She explained the situation, that Rom and Lara Ann, a nice girl he wanted to marry, had come for a visit. They intended to get married, tomorrow, here at the ranch. Could they come?

"If I had an appointment with the president of the United States, I'd cancel it to be there." Nila continued, her voice filled with surprise and excitement. "What do you think they might like for a wedding present?"

"I have no idea, sweetheart, but you'll think of something. You're good at that."

"Alright, I'll give it some thought. Are they staying long for their visit with you and Pete at the ranch?"

"I don't know, but I doubt it. I'm guessing they probably have to rush back to Oklahoma and their jobs riding for the 101. Odd, they haven't mentioned that, but we've not had much time to talk. They are in

Skiddy right now getting their marriage license, finding a minister to conduct the ceremony, and will be stopping to pick up Andy who has stayed over at the Webbers'. I wouldn't be surprised if Rom takes a few minutes to visit friends while he's in that neighborhood and asks them to come to his wedding."

They talked too long, visiting, and Jocelyn had just put away her iron and ironing board and was setting out the ingredients for a cake when Andy hit the door and burst in. "Rom brought me home, Ma," he declared at the top of his voice. "An' he's going to be here with us."

"Yes he is, honey, at least for his wedding tomorrow. I'm as glad as you to see him and to meet Lara Ann, his bride. She's nice, isn't she?"

His face flooded red, along with a smirky, embarrassed grin. "She kissed me."

"Oh, my goodness, she did?"

"Rom asked me to be his 'groom man' whatever that is. When I said yes, she kissed me."

"You'd make a wonderful groomsman, wait and see." Jocelyn was reaching for a bowl on the cupboard shelf to make the wedding cake just as Lara Ann and Rom came in arms filled with bundles.

"Good heavens, what is all this?" Jocelyn waited with hands on her hips.

Rom grinned, his eyes shining. "To start with, flowers for my bride, a boutonniere for me. Six dozen doughnuts from the bakery, they said 'pile 'em like a cake and stick a posy in the top.' And that's what we're going to do."

"I was just about to bake you a cake, Son."

He shrugged. "Well, you're not." He blew her a kiss. "As I was saying, we got a pretty new dress for Lara

Ann, and new trousers and shirt for me. Flowers for you, too, Mom. Sandwich fixins that guests can make themselves, and candy and nuts. Extra cream and bananas to make homemade ice cream. Other stuff."

"Maybe it's none of my business, Rom, but where did you get the money for all that?" Jocelyn waved her hand, rubbed her cheek, completely flustered. "I thought the wedding was going to be simple." *Cheap*.

This time, Lara Ann answered. She suppressed a giggle, her expression quickly turning serious. "Our good friends at the 101 Ranch, from those who work on the ranch to the large number of folks who perform in their rodeos, passed a hat when they heard we were getting married. That's from a lot of folks, more than one hat, and we tried to stop them."

Rom entered the conversation. "Even finally getting them to stop, it's enough money to buy ten fine horses and a decent-sized herd of cattle."

Jocelyn cupped her chin in her palm. "This is a joke, isn't it?"

"No joke. Just a minute, Ma. When we get our stuff unloaded, you'll have your flowers. Need to get 'em in water."

When the unloading was finished, food items going into the icebox on the porch, flowers in jars of water, clothes to the bedrooms, Rom turned to Jocelyn, and Pete, who'd just come to the house for a cup of coffee. "Ma, Pop, we'd like for you to stand up with us in our wedding ceremony. Be Lara Ann's matron of honor and my best man. Alright with you two?"

Jocelyn found it hard for her to speak over a lump forming in her throat. Tears sprang to her eyes. "Y-y-yes, if that's what you want."

"Hey, yes, I'm honored." Pete shook Rom's hand. "Now then, I have to finish this cup of coffee and get back to work."

"I'm coming with you to help." Rom kissed Lara Ann's cheek and when Pete set his empty cup on the table, followed him outside.

~

The next day Jocelyn was saying, "You're an angel, Nila, coming today to help with the wedding and allowing me time to cuddle our sweet baby April." She bounced the baby in her arms, parading through the kitchen while Nila stacked doughnuts, adding a dab of icing so that they would stay in place to form the 'wedding cake.'

"I couldn't wait to get here." Nila turned with a smile. "I had to be part of the fixings and see my chosen brother, Rom, get married."

"I'll never forget how the two of you ended up part of our family and dearly loved. Rommy and his father had come to live near us. Rom, a young boy going to our local school. Trouble came up, and they had to quit our part of the country. Rom's father had stolen a rancher's steer to ward off him and his boy starving. He was wrongly accused of doing much more than that and threatened with hanging." She patted the baby's back, silent for a few moments. "We helped send the two of them back to where they'd come from, in Nebraska. Rom returned to us later, a very sick boy. After he recovered, he strongly insisted on staying with us for good at Nickel Hill, rather than being with his father, on the run. And you, Nila, turned out of your family by your mother, because you refused to marry the elderly well-to-do man she picked for you."

Nila washed her hands in a pan of water and dried them. "Ah, yes, my dear mother, Flaudie Malone back then, remarried now to Rom's father. She was so sure there had to've been a will when her aunt Letty died. Your grandma Letty."

Jocelyn's face sobered. "Your mother just wouldn't listen to the truth, the facts."

"I was so ashamed when she insisted that you took over, *stole* the ranch without telling her about a will." Nila shook her head. "Such nonsense."

"Farfetched for sure. We were only managers of Nickel Hill at that time. And my grandma had little to nothing to leave in a will, let alone a ranch." She gently snuggled the sleeping baby closer on her shoulder. "I have to say, Pete and I've never regretted a moment that your mother insisted we take you and provide for you. It's been one of the best things to ever happen to us."

"And to me. Say, has the preacher arrived yet? Don't want this cake to get melty and topple after I've put the little bouquet of pretty prairie primroses on top."

"He's here, outside meeting with Rom and Pete, being shown where the ceremony will be held."

"Where will that be?"

"Rom and Lara Ann agreed that their wedding should be held in the shade of the orchard. In a pretty spot with peach trees still blooming. Everything is turning out nicer than I thought it might, Nila. The men set up a table in the orchard, where the doughnut cake and apple cider will be served. Another table for sandwiches, candy, and nuts. A later treat of banana ice cream." Jocelyn handed sleeping baby April to Nila when she reached for her. "The wedding will begin anytime now." For a moment, her breath caught. "Shhh, look, there's Lara Ann coming downstairs. My goodness, she's beautiful."

From Lara Ann's shoulders on down, the high neck, bouffant sleeved dress was row upon row of delicate white lace ruffles. She carried a wide, long satiny, cream-colored sash. "Would you help me with this, please, Mrs. Pladson? It goes around my waist and is tied in a big bow in back, with long ends of the sash trailing down."

"Your dress is so beautiful, like you, Lara Ann, that I'm almost afraid to touch it. But yes, come here, and I'll tie it for you."

"For sure," Nila said quietly. "Pretty as a picture. Love your small beaded hair piece of creamy rose buds, white baby's breath, and green leaves. Beautiful on your long, shiny brown curls. They match your dress perfectly." She stepped lightly away. "Now I need to put this babe down for her nap. Look...out there." She nodded toward the window. "There are folks heading toward the orchard already."

"I hope I haven't held things up, I'd better hurry." Lara Ann gathered her skirts in one hand, her other hand holding her hair piece in place, and rushed toward the back door.

Jocelyn followed, needing to find Andy, already dressed for his groomsman part—however that would turn out. Knowing him, he could be down to the crick with other boys who'd arrived, their pants legs rolled up and wading. Muddied, a possibility.

NINETEEN

Jocelyn arrived at the orchard in time to see Mabel Goody twisting this way and that with a finger to her lips for silence. The minister smiled, waited for the group of guests to halt their chatter, and began. "We are gathered here today to rejoice in one of life's most beautiful moments, the joining of two hearts. To give recognition to the significance and beauty of love. To add our best wishes to the words which shall unite this couple in marriage. The remarkable has happened. They met each other, fell in love, and are securing that attachment with their wedding. A good marriage must be fondly created."

He spoke fifteen minutes or more, giving points of advice. Ending with, "It is keeping in mind to say 'I love you' every day. This is not only joining life with the right person, it's being the right partner. And now your vows." He nodded for Rom to speak his part.

He took Lara Ann's hands in his. "I, Romney Trey-hern, take you, Lara Ann Yost, to be my wife, my partner in life, and my one true love. I will cherish our friendship and love you with all my heart through all time."

Lara Ann's eyes sparkled with adoration as they met Rom's happy expression. "I, Lara Ann Yost, take you, Romney Treyhern, to be my husband, my partner in life, and my one true love. I will cherish our friendship and love you with all my heart through all time."

The minister met their look of expectancy. He began, "Romney Treyhern, do you take Lara Ann Yost to be your wife?"

"I sure do."

"Lara Ann Yost, do you take Romney Treyhern to be your husband?"

She moistened her lips. "I do."

"The rings?" The minister waited.

Romney turned to Pete, holding out his hand, and Pete, wearing a wide grin, gave him the ring. Rom very carefully put the ring on Lara Ann's finger. "This ring is my gift, with my promise that I will always love you, cherish you, and honor you all the days of my life. And with this ring, I thee wed."

Lara Ann took the groom's ring from Jocelyn with a smile of thanks and turned to Rom, saying softly, as though her husband-to-be was the only other person present. "This ring is my gift, with my promise that I will always love you, cherish you, and honor you all the days of my life. With this ring, I thee wed."

"By the power in me, I now pronounce you man and wife, Mr. and Mrs. Treyhern. You may kiss." Beaming, he said to the guests, "I present to you our happy couple."

Jocelyn wiped tears and laughed softly. She turned

and hugged Rom, then Lara Ann. "My goodness, Rom, you're a married man, in a sweet ceremony, too. And such a dear wife, to boot. Congratulations, you two. I predict you'll have a wonderful life."

"Thanks, Mrs. Pladson." Lara Ann kissed Jocelyn's cheek.

Rom, flushing, did likewise. "Thanks, Ma. For all you've done for me. For us." He shook Pete's hand as Pete clapped his shoulder. "And you, too, Pa."

Jocelyn and Pete moved aside to let others congratulate the newlyweds. They chatted a bit with those in waiting in line, and invited them to the food table.

Though the wedding ceremony was short, the celebration of Rom and Lara Ann's marrying was the opposite. Relaxed visiting hummed here and there in the shade of the orchard. Rom's doughnut cake and apple cider was praised over and over, luckily there were more doughnuts that didn't go into the cake, and plenty of cider. The ham sandwiches were relished by all, as were the candy and nut treats. After visiting with other guests, Rom came to sit with Jocelyn and Pete, a sandwich in one hand and a doughnut in the other. Jocelyn chuckled. "Your wedding is successful, Rom, no question about it. Your visit has been such fun, this celebration topping it. I suppose you and your pretty wife will be heading back to Oklahoma and your jobs tomorrow? We'll be on the road to Council Grove in the morning, early. We're to be witnesses there, against the Scott brothers in their trial. Hope to never see those ruffians again after that, ever."

Rom shook his head. "Ma, we don't aim to go back. We're here to stay."

"Excuse me, say that again." Pete gave Rom a surprised look. Jocelyn was too shocked to speak.

Rom threw back his head and laughed. "I'm sorry. I guess I should have told you as soon as we got here. We didn't come to only visit, get married and leave. We came *home*. I want to help you run the ranch, Pa. And Lara Ann would be here to help Ma with her work." He rubbed the center of his forehead, his eyes closed, then opened to look closely at Pete and Jocelyn. "We hoped that before long you'd sell us a portion of the acreage so we can build a home of our own, raise a family—like you have."

Having heard Rom, his young wife walked over, standing at his shoulder. "He's been homesick most of the time we've worked together at the 101 Ranch." She reached for his hand and held it. "His dream was always to be here. Come home to live."

Rom's brow wrinkled in a slight frown. "If you can't do that—take me in as partner and sell us a piece of land —we'll still be settling here in Morris County."

Jocelyn finally got her breath back. "Merciful heavens, *yes*, Rom. We'd give anything to have you here with us, wouldn't we, Pete?" She moved closer to him.

"Sounds to me like it's already settled and as far as I'm concerned, it's a damn good deal." Pete reached over and shook Rom's hand. "You two pick the acreage you want, and it's yours."

Jocelyn could hardly wait to share the news with Nila, who'd come over to them, holding baby April close. Nila hugged Jocelyn's shoulder with her free arm. "Caught the end of you all's conversation, and I think it's wonderful. Nor am I surprised. You need one another and it'll be fine. Just wanted to tell you that I have to get back to Topeka before the sun goes down and it gets too dark to drive the Buick."

"I'll see you off." Jocelyn gathered her skirts in hand and hurried along with Nila.

"Me, too." Lara Ann caught up with them.

When Jocelyn and Lara Ann had returned to the yard, others drifted by, thanking Jocelyn and Pete for a pleasant time. Several congratulated the newlyweds again, adding advice for the days ahead in their marriage. Some serious suggestions. Others joking and causing a round of laughter.

The remaining guests were held up a few more minutes while Pete stood aside with the men, and Jocelyn with the women, letting them know that Rom and Lara Ann were now part of the Nickel Hill Ranch outfit. Bringing on more congratulations.

Hours later, climbing into bed alongside Pete, who was beginning to snore, Jocelyn was worn out but happy. It had been a very good day, a day of joy, and the blessed good news that Rom and his wife, Lara Ann, were here to be partners in running the ranch. Both knew horses and cattle well, a godsend. They'd be living close when their babies came, and grew up right here on Nickel Hill Ranch. And here with Andy while they had to be gone, like tomorrow when they had to go to Council Grove.

We could enjoy the next few days so much, if it weren't for that shuddersome Scott Brother's trial taking our time.

They had left home before dawn and were nearing Council Grove when four riders came pounding hard out of the distance toward them, bringing a dust cloud toward them.

"What in the dickens?"

Pete pulled their team and wagon off to the side of the road, out of the way. To Jocelyn's shock, as three of the riders raced past them, she recognized Dillard Scott and his two brothers. Rowena came next, riding hard.

"Wait!" Jocelyn shouted. "Rowena, what is this? What happened?"

Rowena slowed, pulled up her mount for a few seconds, her expression determined. "You'll find the marshal and his wife on up the road. Not too far out of Council Grove. They need your help. I didn't intend to shoot the marshal. I don't know enough about guns to put on a postage stamp, but I needed to have a gun as a threat, to make the marshal and his wife let my brothers go. The marshal was trying to wrest it from my hand when it went off and wounded him in his left thigh." She had a haunted look. "They can tell you the rest."

"Rowena, for pity's sake, what have you done?" *What about the trial?* Jocelyn stood up in the wagon, getting ready to climb out. Rowena motioned her back.

"I'm taking my brothers to California, or Kentucky, maybe, the way I planned. I'm going to set them up in business, give them a chance to go straight, but there will be no trial." Her horse tossed its head, jerking and dancing in an effort to move on and Rowena yanked on the reins. "I'll see to it that the first earnings they get will go to you folks, they'll be repaying you for all they did to you."

When Jocelyn started to speak again, Rowena held up a hand. "I know you might not believe it, but they want what I have to offer, badly enough to go straight. If they ever try to harm anyone again, I'll turn them over to the law, myself. They know it." Riding off, she turned to shout, "Don't try to follow. It'll do you no good. We'll be in Skiddy and on the train before you could catch us." In a fraction of time, she'd disappeared in a cloud of dust.

Jocelyn sat back down on the wagon seat. "Did that just happen?"

"Yep." Pete shook the lines over the team. "We better find the marshal, and Cora, wherever he is ahead, before he bleeds to death."

A few miles farther on, they spotted the marshal's wagon, small in the distance ahead. When they arrived, they found Cora seated on the ground, the marshal's head in her lap.

The left leg of his trousers had been torn away from the bloody wound. Fortunately, his thigh had the neckerchief Cora had been wearing earlier wrapped tight around it to stop the bleeding. Jocelyn leaped from the wagon and hurried over. She kneeled on the ground next to them. "How is he?" She touched Cora's arm. "How is Leo?" He looked to be passed out. She hoped it was only that he'd gone to sleep.

"For one thing, mad as hell at that woman and her brothers for what they've done to us. Other than that, his thigh has a flesh wound that needs sewing up by a doctor as soon as we can get on to Council Grove and can find one. I've got the bleeding mostly stopped. While we're there, we can also inform the judge and lawyers, the jury, there will be no trial today."

Pete stood by with a canvas water bag. "You folks have a drink of water and then we'll get you, Leo"—whose eyes had opened—"into the wagon and on to Council Grove." He squatted and held the water bag to the marshal's lips.

Cora took the next drink. "Thank the skies you two are here. We hoped you'd be following, not ahead of us already in Council Grove." She handed the water bag back to Pete. "Now let's get Leo into the wagon and on to a doctor."

Marshal Hillis had a second drink. "W-wish it was whiskey. H-hurts like hell." He struggled to sit up straighter.

"Sorry." Pete shook his head. "I don't have any with me. We're going to leave your wagon here for now. We'll find a way to get it back to you later."

"Alright, Pete." He groaned. "I-I got some things in the wagon—blankets, rope, my rifle. I'd like you to take the stuff with us in your wagon, in case someone with—with sticky fingers comes along."

"Sure, I'll do that. First, let's get you into our wagon. We need to be on our way quick as we can. You've bled enough."

As the wagon rolled on, Pete pushing the team to hurry, the Hillises told what happened. "We-we had the three Scott outlaws in our wagon, handcuffed and legs tied," Marshal Hillis spoke from where he lay on a pile of blankets behind the other three seated above him. "Everything as it should be. Then suddenly it—it all blew up." He spoke as if he couldn't believe his words.

"We spotted horses ahead, and when we got up to them, a woman stepped out with a gun in her hand, ordering us to free our prisoners." Cora sighed heavily. "We saw then that it was their sister. Rowena Scott's her name? She had four horses with her, must have herded them there before dawn, and waited for us to come by."

"By no way was I going to let her take them three fellas from us." The marshal's voice was harsh. "I jumped off our wagon and grabbed to get her gun from her. She hung on to it tight, wouldn't let it go. I had to wrestle for it like hell and that's when the gun went off. Hit me."

"She looked sorry for it," Cora said. "But still held the gun on us."

"An' I'd landed on my left side, my gun under me." The marshal cleared his throat. "I didn't give a hockey stick about the pain, but couldn't move fast like I wanted."

Cora fanned herself, agitation in her expression. "I'd drawn my gun by then, and stood up in the wagon, ordering the sister to drop hers."

Marshal Hillis scowled. "One of the prisoners close behind where Cora was, the biggest one, somehow got to his feet quicker'n scat and threw his whole body against Cora, knocking her off the wagon, her gun flying from her hand far into the rocks and brush."

"I reached desperately for my gun under me, feeling mad enough to kill somebody but couldn't get to it. The sister came over to where I was lying on the ground, bleeding like hell, and made me give her the keys to her brothers' handcuffs. Apologizing, can you beat that? Damn woman freed the one first that hit Cora. Then he freed the others. They were all scrambling then to get their legs untied."

Cora's voice thickened. "They were out of here practically flying away on those horses, and we couldn't do one thing about it." A moment of dead silence followed.

"They were long gone before I could get my gun from under me."

"To Skiddy and the train," Jocelyn spoke up. "They rode past us as we were headed this way."

"Can you believe the sister apologized to us again before she rode off?" Cora rubbed absently at her arms.

Jocelyn didn't answer but gave Cora's question a thought. *Yes, I do believe she'd apologize. She wouldn't be happy to have done anything to you two, in the process of reclaiming her brothers. That was Rowena. Desperate to the point of risking her own life to save her brothers, but kind to the law folk she was stealing them from.*

Marshal Hillis shifted his good leg slightly from where he lay in the back of the wagon. "I'll try to track 'em down as soon as I can travel on this injured leg, but the truth is, I'm glad to have them out of my hands. That Rowena, their sister, promised that if her criminal brothers don't follow her orders and change their ways, she'll bring them back to me." His voice was weakening as he added, "And I believe she would."

As much as she'd wanted to be friends with Rowena, Jocelyn was thinking, *it'd probably never happen now.* And possibly for the better, although she'd always have admiration, in a way, for Rowena's spunk.

When they reached Council Grove and were passing the courthouse, Pete dropped Jocelyn off, the marshal ordering, "You explain to the lawyers and Judge Rawlins, and those on the jury, why there ain't no trial, Mrs. Pladson. Or they can come talk to me over to the doctor's when he's taking care of my leg." He gave a painful sigh. "Get me on to the doctor, Pete. Sure glad you found us when you did. That Rowena said you'd help us in time."

At the courthouse, Jocelyn went over her explanation for the third time, speaking to lawyers, probable jurists, and now Judge Rawlins who'd just shown up. "Yes, Your Honor, as Marshal Hillis and his wife Cora told us, the prisoners' sister, Rowena Scott, laid in wait for Marshal Hillis and Deputy Cora. Stepped out from among the horses she'd brought and held a gun on Marshal Hillis and his wife. When the marshal tried to get Rowena's gun away from her, she held on tight as death. In the struggle between them, the gun went off, the bullet into his thigh. Not a serious wound that'd kill him but bad enough to keep him from trying to stop them. Pete and the marshal's wife have the marshal at the doctor's office." She sighed, hated in some way to reveal so much about the woman she'd wanted as a friend. "Slick as silk, Cora said while she was frantically searching for her gun that landed somewhere in rocks and brush, Rowena badgered the hurt marshal into giving her the keys to their handcuffs. Crazy fast, they were freed and off on the horses their sister brought them to ride."

"I'm glad the marshal wasn't killed." The judge rubbed his jaw, his expression glum. "I suppose we should send a few lawmen after them, but the sister was probably right in saying it'd do no good, they'd be gone and to god knows where. We'll see." His expression cleared somewhat. "They hadn't committed murder, and most of their other doings were of lower regard."

"Their sister said that after she sees the brothers employed, the first money they earned would go to us, pay us back for the trouble they caused." She told the judge, lawyers, and others, "Marshal Hillis indicated he was just glad to be rid of them. At the moment he felt that way." Jocelyn looked down at her feet, then up, chin lifted. "Pete and I feel pretty much the same. As long as the Scott brothers are out of our lives, we're satisfied."

Judge Rawlins nodded. "So be it, then. No trial. No big hunt for the minor lawbreakers. Now, I need to get back to my office. Nice to see you again, Jocelyn, regardless of the situation bringing us together."

"Nice seeing you, too, Judge Rawlins."

She walked to the doctor's office and found the doctor and Marshal Hillis in the midst of an argument.

"Stay here in the hospital?" the marshal growled. "I'm not in that bad of a way. No sir! We're going over to the Hays House restaurant for a quick meal, since we had no breakfast, then we're heading home. Only five or six hours from now we'll be back to Skiddy. It's summer, the sun won't be going down for hours yet. I can roll up in a blanket in the wagon and sleep on the way. We'll be home before dark, and if we don't, we have a lantern to see by."

Jocelyn gave Pete a look of distress. His mouth quirked and his shoulder lifted. Then he winked at her. "Gotta do what the law orders, I reckon."

"Sure you do," Marshall Hillis said. "Right, wife?"

Cora frowned. "If you say so, sweetheart. We'll go home yet today."

The doctor, an older gray-haired man wearing a deep frown, threw his hands up. "Alright, have your way. I'll send crutches with you to help you get around."

"I don't need crutches. I've still got one leg and I can limp a little on the other with no harm done. Thank you, Doc. Now what's the bill?"

TWENTY

"I love this place," Jocelyn said, looking around as the foursome waited for their meal of Berkshire pork pot roast, sweet potatoes, baked beans, and sliced apples. She looked at the others, Marshal Hillis, who was being extra careful with his leg, Cora tending to him, and Pete—seated next to her at the table. To get their minds off their troubles, she continued, "I suppose you all know that the Hays House restaurant and trading post dates back a long way, to around 1857?" She sipped her iced tea. "For years, this was a popular stopping place right along the Santa Fe Trail for traders taking goods from Missouri to New Mexico. Thanks to Seth Hays, grandson of Daniel Boone, for building Hays House. He'd chiefly come to Council Grove with his cousin, A.G. Boone, to trade with the Kaw Indians."

"Yup, he did. And he sold everything from guns and blankets to flour and tinware, to them Indians and others." Marshal Hillis took a drink of the beer he'd ordered and waved his hand in a circling motion. "This was a tavern, too, always has been." He motioned his head toward the bar with the huge mirror behind it and the stone fireplace.

Cora arranged the plates and eating utensils the server brought to the table. "As I've heard, for years this building has served as a trading post, courthouse, post office, printing office, meeting and social hall. And some years, rooms to rent upstairs."

"Hays House is the pride of Council Grove, and no wonder..." Jocelyn sat with her hand on her stomach, feeling starved. A short while later, their steaming plates of food were served, and all conversation ended.

The drive back to Skiddy would be long, but turned out pleasant enough due to conversation. Marshal Hillis was as comfortable as they could manage, rolled up in a blanket. Off and on, he was telling them about the young deputy he'd borrowed from White City to take his and Cora's place while they were gone. He could be having all kinds of trouble. Or not, if he were lucky. He finally drifted off to sleep but moaned with pain the few times that he moved.

Jocelyn, Cora, and Pete discussed the matter of Rowena Scott and the action she'd taken to save her brothers. "I would've never dreamed she'd do such a thing. She's not a bad person, herself," Jocelyn lamented. She rubbed her brow, struggling to find the right words. "How hard it must've been, for a person like her, to work up the courage to pull off the deed."

"In a way, it's not a bad thing that she did," Pete said. "She wants to turn her brothers around, get them on the right road, make something good of themselves. Can't blame her for that."

Cora spoke quietly. "I don't think Leo, marshal to you folks, minds all that much that they've been taken off our hands. I don't mind. Those rascals were nothing but meanness to me while they were in our jail. Almost made me want to hang them some days. Or turn them loose." She laughed at her joke.

The next couple hours passed in silence. Behind them, lying in the wagon, Marshal Hillis stirred. "Aren't we there yet?"

Pete answered. "Gettin' close. We'll have you there, sleeping in your own bed, before you know it."

"And we'll make sure Doc Ashwood is over to see you first thing in the morning." Cora was stern. "I want his opinion, Leo, about how much it's alright for you to be up and around. You know I can take over from the borrowed deputy, keep law and order as good as you and him together."

The marshal spoke, admiration in his tone. "Can't argue with that, Cora darlin'. You done good in your job many a time. Best deputy I'll ever have."

For the last several miles, everyone was quiet. Finally nearing Skiddy, Jocelyn noted a trail of smoke in the blue sky ahead. She spoke, mostly to herself aloud, "There it is, the train the three culprits, and maybe their sister, Rowena, too, were going to be on."

"Well, they had time to be there, so they probably are on that train, going wherever it is they figured on." Pete laced his fingers behind his head, his eyes half-closed in satisfaction.

"I'm glad." Jocelyn reached over and took the lines that lay in Pete's lap, feeling a sense of relief that she hadn't had for a long while. "I'm ready for some peace, but mostly happy that the Scott brothers have finally recognized, and they surely have—that Nickel Ranch is ours, legally and for sure, and can't by any means be taken from us."

A short while later, they were in Skiddy, parking in front of the Hillis home. The couple's older children, a young man and a girl, came out to meet them. They stared at the three sitting up in the wagon. "Where's Pa?" the girl asked.

"Right here in the durn wagon, muffin." The marshal struggled to a sitting position, wincing with pain.

"Don't move, Marshal, until we can help you down from the wagon." Jocelyn was off the seat and around to the side of the wagon like it was on fire. She reached out and patted him. "So sorry this has happened to you, Marshal Hillis. I hope your wound heals in a hurry and the pain eases considerably in the meantime."

He laughed, the sound of it edged with pain. "Thanks, Jocelyn. I hope to holy heaven I get what you want."

His wife and children had little trouble getting him from the wagon, his feet on the ground, and crippling toward the house. He waved a 'thank you' behind his head to Jocelyn and Pete.

"You're welcome, Marshal." She was feeling better about him now that he was home with family, and Doc Ashwood's office and hospital only a few paces down the street. "We'll be checking on you. Take care and get well."

Cora waved, and the door closed behind them.

Pete put his arm around Jocelyn's waist. "C'mon,

honey. We still got a ways to go."

Back in the wagon and on their way, she turned to him. "It's alright, isn't it? Everything that's happened since we left home early this morning—that seems like ages ago? The upside-down-ness of it all?"

"It can stay that way, as far as I'm concerned, sweetheart. We have our own life to tend to, don't you think? I know I got other plans."

As their wagon rumbled along, the rosy sun lowering in the west, Jocelyn's thoughts turned to the past. Finally, she spoke. "You know, Pete, when I was a young girl, teased to death at school about my cleft mouth, I was sure I'd never have a normal life. That my grandma Letty and my father would be the only ones who'd ever truly love me. Besides the two of them, you were the neighbor boy who accepted me just the way I was before I had surgery that repaired my mouth. Then my grandma died, and then my father, after losing our farm to the bank. That part was hard as the dickens."

Pete lowered his head to kiss her cheek. His thumb wiping her tears.

"You know the rest," she went on to say. "We met again at that rodeo where you were competing. We fell in love even deeper than the attachment we had when we were teenagers. Got married, have a beautiful ranch. A young son we wouldn't trade anything in the world for, and two other children who found us and became our family. Both married now, Nila and John and their baby girl. Rom and Lara Ann becoming our partners on the ranch." She wiped her eyes. "We're so lucky, Pete."

"That we are."

She was quiet a few minutes as Pete pulled her closer. She looked up at him. "Pete, I want you to know that for all I thought my life would be, I'm the happiest woman in the whole wide world."

"The *whole world*?" Pete laughed, his lips brushing her brow.

"Alright, the happiest, luckiest woman in the *Kansas Flint Hills*. Will that do?"

"It'll do, it'll do."

~

Six blissful but busy weeks passed. Half of Nickel Hill Ranch, ten thousand acres, were put in Rom and Lucy Trayhern's name. They were partners, work-wise, everything about running the ranch, after all. In rare free time, Rom was building a small house for them up the road from Jocelyn and Pete's home. According to Lara Ann, from the moment she and Rom decided to get married, they'd both put away part of their earnings from the 101 Ranch. They had a nice little savings between them. In time, they could borrow from the bank if they had to, but both Rom and Lara Ann were against the idea. Earnings from the ranch could now be increased, from putting in more crops raised to sell, breeding larger herds of cattle and horses. Andy loved being in the middle of it all, and was showing signs of being a rancher, or cowboy, someday himself.

Jocelyn stopped short, humming *Red River Valley* when she opened the mailbox and saw the flat square package. It was addressed to her and Pete, but there was no return address, or name. She should wait to open it after her day's work was done, but curiosity got the better of her. Back in the kitchen at the table, humming *Red River Valley* again, she opened the package with care. Photos and a folded newspaper were inside a heavy paper envelope. She slowly drew them out.

Her breath caught, looking at the first large photograph that featured a three-part building made of unpainted boards but tidy and neat. The middle section was two stories high with outside stairs going up and a wide balcony around it. Other doors led from the level ground into attached buildings. She clapped a hand to her mouth when she read the sign over the door, *SMITH BROTHERS BREWERY, SALOON, AND STEAK HOUSE* and saw the three men standing out front. Admittedly, they looked like fine, well-dressed, clean-shaven, prosperous businessmen. But clearly from their faces, they were Dillard Scott and his two brothers.

"She's done it. She did, just like she said she wanted, and they wanted. It's happened."

"Who did what, Jocelyn?" Lara Ann turned from the sink where she was peeling peaches for a cobbler. "You sound pretty worked up. Anything wrong?"

"Yes, no, not really wrong, I suppose. The Scott brothers, who tried every cruel act to try and get Nickel Hill Ranch from us, have changed their name to Smith. They've gone into business. Their sister, Rowena, provided the money. I don't know exactly where this is located. There's no way to tell from looking at these pictures. Wait, here's a newspaper." She opened it, scanned the top, and read aloud, "*RAWLINGS WEEKLY TIMES*. No state is mentioned. It could be anywhere from California to Kentucky. Arizona or Idaho. I don't know." She read slowly. "Ah me, they are glorifying and giving a big hand of thanks to the three Smith brothers for reopening this vacated business.

Only thing wrong with that is they are the three *Scott hoodlums*."

She propped her head up with her fist and, with her other hand, tapped her fingers on the table in chagrin. "Anyhow, that's who they were a month or so ago. Smith is not their real name." She sighed, shaking her head. Lara Ann already knew enough about the Scott brothers to explain anything more.

When Pete came in for supper, Jocelyn showed him the pictures and the newspaper.

"What do you think?"

He shrugged and looked tired from a long day's work. "I think we're darned lucky. You know, with things so fine for them, I doubt if they'll commit any crimes wherever they are now. If they did, they'd be kept there, no bother to us." He looked to be giving the subject more thought, scratching the side of his nose. "Maybe, just maybe, they'll be successful with their three businesses and the future will be great for them. For us as well here in Kansas, away from their fool plan to take our ranch." He looked at her. "If we ever find out where their businesses are, let's go visit them. Have drinks and supper at their steak house. Shake hands with them."

Jocelyn, wide-eyed, burst out laughing. "You have to be kidding. Really, Pete?"

"It could be a nice little final tie-up to this whole mess. Yep, keep this in mind." He grinned.

"Alright, someday we'll give them a good-natured visit if you say so." She went to sit on his lap, brush his hair back, and give him a loving hug. "In the meantime, though, let's enjoy things just as they are, a heavenly peace since they left Kansas."

A Look At:
The Plainswoman

Award-winning author Irene Bennett Brown's timeless tale of endurance, perseverance, and passion for life.

Amity Whitford dared to stake a claim on the endless plains of western Kansas. She built her homestead, Dove's Nest, with her bare hands in an effort to tame the wild lands and carve out a place of her own. But the ravages of the sun and drying winds took their toll, putting her dreams and her livelihood in dire jeopardy.

Desperate for funds, fiercely independent Amity accepted another challenge–to run for election as the county school superintendent. Her campaign was greeted with disbelief, scorn, open hostility...and interest.

But as her dream came within reach, and her love for local newspaper publisher Chalk Holden dared to bloom in her heart, Amity's past returned, carrying with it a menace more fierce than any storm on the open plains...

AVAILABLE NOW

ABOUT THE AUTHOR

Irene Bennett Brown is an award-winning author who enjoys using Kansas, where she was born, as background for her historical novels for both children and adults. She is a recipient of the Western Writers of America Owen Wister Award, and induction into Western Writers of America Hall of Fame. Other awards include Western Writers of America Spur Award, the Will Rogers Medallion Award, a nomination for the Mark Twain Award and other honors.

She lives with her husband, Bob, a retired research chemist, on two fruitful acres along the Santiam River in Oregon.